Advance prai[illegible]

BAD MEDICINE

by Geoffrey M. Cooper

Brad Parker and Karen Richmond Book 3

"Written in a clear, captivating voice, Cooper draws you in from the very beginning...This is thriller writing at its best; you won't be disappointed."

—*Manhattan Book Review*

"*Bad Medicine* adds another new medical thriller to Geoffrey M. Cooper's arsenal of hard-hitting novels...a compelling read, worthy of acclaim and recommendation."

—*Midwest Book Review*

"Cooper outdoes himself in his latest medical thriller...Realistic, non-stop action, *Bad Medicine* is the ultimate in science suspense novels."

—*Seattle Book Review*

Praise for *Nondisclosure* by Geoffrey M. Cooper
Brad Parker and Karen Richmond Book 1
IndieReader Discovery Award

"*Nondisclosure* is one of the year's best mysteries by a Maine writer...a gritty mystery, well-crafted with a complex, intriguing plot, tense suspense, vivid action and wholly believable characters."

—*Central Maine Sentinel*

"This book manages to accomplish, in a short space, what few books are capable of with far more pages. It is at once a compelling mystery, a fascinating peek into the politics of academia, and a nuanced look at the Me Too movement."

—*Manhattan Book Review*

"Geoffrey M. Cooper crafts a riveting saga of mystery, discovery, and redemption...Readers interested in medical thrillers will relish the turns taken in an engrossing story that's hard to put down."

—*Midwest Book Review*

"A fast-paced medical thriller with a cast full of brilliant characters. Engaging and suspenseful to the very end!"

—*San Francisco Book Review*

"*Nondisclosure* is a highly recommended read for fans of politically charged murder mysteries, thrilling suspense novels, and current social issues."

—*Readers' Favorite*

"[A]n intriguing and meticulously plotted medical thriller that involves the inner workings at a top research university where scandal threatens to taint its important new discovery."

—*IndieReader*

"*Nondisclosure* successfully continues in the same vein as *The Prize* as a story of murder and deceit in the world of scientific research and academia...*Nondisclosure* is an outstanding murder mystery, one that should help Geoffrey M. Cooper continue to make a name for himself as an intelligent, thoroughly entertaining writer."

—*Colorado Book Review*

Praise for *Forever* by Geoffrey M. Cooper
Brad Parker and Karen Richmond Book 2
Readers' Favorite Gold Medal

"Complete with science, espionage, and action, *Forever* is a book that will keep you on your toes. This is a page-turner from start to finish."

—*San Francisco Book Review*

"[A] gripping, science-based story that revolves around manipulation, mutants, and murky situations. *Forever* is designed to keep readers on edge to its satisfying conclusion."

—*Midwest Book Review*

"Espionage, perilous international affairs, and cynicism can all be found in the chilling novel *Forever*. Cooper has delivered another riveting novel to keep you on the edge of your seat!"

—*Manhattan Book Review*

"A persuasive tale of scientific intrigue."

—*Kirkus Reviews*

"Cooper continues to impress with his suspenseful plotting and sharp, uncluttered prose. In *Forever*, he has skillfully given us a double whammy of scientific subversion and deceit intertwined with foreign espionage."

—*Colorado Book Review*

"Geoffrey M. Cooper has written a chilling page-turner in *Forever: A Medical Thriller*. This gripping tale has many unexpected twists and turns, and the ending is unforeseen. It is a captivating read!"

—*Readers' Favorite*

"[A] tight, edge-of-the-seat whodunit recommended for fans of meticulously researched science-based thrillers."

—*IndieReader*

Praise for *The Prize* by Geoffrey M. Cooper
National Indie Excellence Award
Readers' Favorite Book Award

"Fans of Robin Cook–style medical thrillers will relish the interpersonal relationships, drama, and contrast between lab and scientific research special interests...[T]he result is a thoroughly engrossing science odyssey that touches upon social and research issues alike."

—*Midwest Book Review*

"An intense story about ruthlessness in the scientific community."

—*Kirkus Reviews*

"A fast-paced science thriller that would rival Michael Crichton or Patricia Cornwell."

—*Manhattan Book Review*

"Geoffrey M. Cooper creates stunning antagonists in *The Prize*, while peeling back the curtain of the scientific community to reveal its humanity. A great read for science lovers and anyone who enjoys a big, juicy scandal."

—*IndieReader*

"*The Prize* is a clever, suspenseful page-turner for seasoned lab-coat wearers and novice geeks alike."

—*Colorado Book Review*

"A medical thriller at its best...a page-turner that is intelligently plotted and accomplished with unusual finesse and mastery."

—*Readers' Favorite*

"[A] serious account of how scientific investigation can be sidetracked by chicanery...The end spirals to a climax that is only partially predictable."

—*San Francisco Book Review*

BAD MEDICINE

A Medical Thriller

BRAD PARKER AND KAREN RICHMOND BOOK 3

GEOFFREY M. COOPER

Also by Geoffrey M. Cooper

Fiction

The Prize

Nondisclosure: A Medical Thriller
Brad Parker and Karen Richmond Book 1

Forever: A Medical Thriller
Brad Parker and Karen Richmond Book 2

Science

Oncogenes

Elements of Human Cancer

The Cancer Book

The Cell: A Molecular Approach

Bad Medicine

ISBN: 978-1-63381-248-2
eBook ISBN: 978-1-63381-249-9

Designed and produced by:
Maine Authors Publishing
12 High Street, Thomaston, Maine
www.maineauthorspublishing.com

Printed in the United States of America

BAD MEDICINE

1

He pulled the hood of his parka tighter around his face as the two figures on the other side of the street drew closer. The gesture was natural enough. It was a cold night, mid-forties with a light rain falling. Not the nicest weather for late May, but this was Maine and winter was adamant in its refusal to depart. There weren't many people out after midnight on a night like this, but York Community College was nearby, so there were occasionally some students hanging around. Like the two fools across the street. As they came nearer, he could smell the marijuana and see the joint they were passing unsteadily between them. He gave a thin smile of relief. No threat of recognition from these clowns, even if he didn't have his face covered.

Despite the lateness of the hour, there were still a few lights on at his destination. The Maine Translational Research Institute. Not a surprise. It was a busy laboratory facility that housed twenty or so active research groups, each run by a faculty member—a principal investigator—with a staff of technicians, graduate students, and postdoctoral researchers. People here—especially the students and postdocs—sometimes worked odd hours, so there were always a few in their labs or offices. As long as he wasn't spotted, it wouldn't be a problem.

Nonetheless, he was reassured by the feel of the Makarov pistol on his left hip. It wouldn't be needed tonight, but he would have felt naked going out on a job without it. An old friend from years ago—he'd made his first kill with it back when he worked for state security.

Checking to be sure that the jacket hood completely covered his face, he let himself in through the institute's unlocked front door. The lack of security at the place never failed to amaze him. There was a video camera monitoring the entrance, but that was it. He could only imagine that they felt safe because the institute was located in a small town in Maine. If it had been in a real city, there would have been locked doors, security guards, the works. But not here. Nothing except the single camera to monitor traffic in and out.

Idiots.

The lobby was empty but just to be sure he didn't run into anyone, he bypassed the elevator and took the stairs up to the fourth floor. A cautious peek around the corner of the stairwell told him that the lights were on in one of the labs, about halfway down the hall. But the equipment room was immediately adjacent to the stairs, so hopefully that wouldn't be a problem. Unless whoever was working down the hall needed something while he was there. It was enough of a possibility to give him a moment's hesitation, but he'd be quick. An interruption was unlikely, and he'd just have to handle it if necessary.

He pulled on purple latex gloves before he exited the stairwell. Then he ducked into the hall and opened the equipment room door. A quick look around revealed four ultracold freezers on the back wall, behind several tables covered with items of equipment like centrifuges, spectrophotometers, and thermocyclers, which were presumably shared by the four different labs on the floor. Using his phone as a flashlight, he went over and examined the freezers. Each was designated as the property of one of the principal investigators. One was conveniently marked C. Gelman, PI. The others were labeled with the names of Davis, Cohen, and Robbins—presumably the other three PIs on the floor. Nice and simple.

He knelt down and turned off the battery-powered alarm switch at the bottom of the Gelman lab freezer. It was set to go off and send a signal to the maintenance office if the freezer lost power or if the temperature rose ten degrees above its setting of minus eighty degrees Centigrade—the one safety measure they actually had in place. But now the alarm wouldn't be a problem. Then he unplugged the freezer from its emergency power circuit and cracked the door open. As long as no one happened to discover it in the next three or four hours, the contents would be ruined.

Making sure the hall was empty, he took the stairs back down to the ground floor, pulled the hood over his head, and left the building unobserved.

A job well done. According to the boss, losing the samples in that freezer would destroy Gelman's study. Enough to put the bitch out of business.

Nonetheless, he had a nagging feeling that more would be needed before his work was done. This little errand couldn't be the whole story. There had to be more for the boss to have brought in someone with his special set of skills.

2

The granite and glass façade of Boston Technological Institute's Central Administration Building—otherwise known as the Presidential Palace—gleamed as brightly as ever. It was an impressive building, designed to let visitors know that they'd arrived at the power center of a major university. I'd worn my best suit two years ago when I first visited it for a private meeting with the former president, Kenneth Emerson. But the sense of grandeur I'd felt on that occasion had worn thin by my second visit, when Karen and I had the pleasure of arresting Emerson for obstruction of justice and hauling him out in handcuffs for his role in the Mike Singer case.

I'd been chair of BTI's Department of Integrated Life Sciences when Singer, a leading professor in my department, had assaulted and subsequently murdered a student. The dean had asked me to help university detective Karen Richmond untangle the sordid mess, which had ended with Singer in prison and Emerson being fired for attempting to cover up Singer's crimes. It had been a sad and ugly affair that had tarnished BTI's reputation and soured me on academic politics. The only good thing was that it had brought me together with Karen.

My former boss, Claire Houghton, had been elevated from her position as dean to take Emerson's place as president of BTI. I liked her. She was smart, honest, and I'd always found her easy to work with. A welcome change from Emerson. But my dealings with him hadn't left me with much respect for the office of the president. Which probably explained why I was dressed in nothing more formal than my usual lab outfit of jeans and a short-sleeved cotton shirt for today's meeting with President Houghton.

I felt pleasantly out of place as I crossed the Palace's marble lobby, filled with busy-looking men and women in business suits, and took the elevator to the top floor. The receptionist outside the Office of the President looked at me as if I were a lost deliveryman. When she finally said, "Can I help you?" her tone indicated that the only thing she wanted to help me with was finding the nearest exit.

I gave her my vain attempt at a winning smile. "I'm Brad Parker. I have a ten o'clock appointment with President Houghton."

She raised a skeptical eyebrow and looked me up and down. "You're Professor Parker?"

I broadened my smile. "That's me."

"Oh. Well then, welcome. The President said I should bring you right in."

She got up and I followed her to an unmarked mahogany door behind the reception desk. It had previously borne a gaudy brass plate announcing that it was the Office of the President, Kenneth Emerson. A touch that the current occupant apparently felt was unnecessary.

The interior of the office had also changed since my last visit. It was still enormous, of course, and the two glass walls with breathtaking views of the Charles River and downtown Boston were still there. But the dark wood paneling on the interior walls had been replaced with a lighter shade, and colorful abstract paintings hung in place of the portraits of former BTI presidents that had been there when Emerson occupied the office. The transformation was completed by the substitution of comfortable-looking modern furniture for the dark, heavy chairs and tables I remembered from Emerson's day. A different office for a different president.

While I was taking it all in, Claire Houghton got up from her desk and walked across the room to greet me with a smile.

"It's good to see you, Brad. It's been a while. Do you like what I've done with the office? Changed a bit from your last visit, hasn't it?"

Observant as ever, she'd noticed me looking around. "It has indeed," I said. "Much for the better. I wouldn't want to be sexist and say that you've given it a woman's touch, but you've certainly made it more open and friendly."

She snorted. "Woman's touch, bullshit! But I'm glad you like it. I wanted to get rid of as much of Emerson's filth as I could."

I nodded. "You succeeded. I especially like that you ditched the portraits of ex-presidents. No need for Emerson to have a place on the wall."

"He wouldn't have had one anyway. But what I have now are examples of the work of our students in the School of Fine Arts. The dean over there sends me a rotating selection every semester."

I took another look—they were good. "I'm impressed; our students do nice work."

She shrugged. "Some of them aren't bad. And it's a good thing to have in the office of a university president, don't you think? Especially when parents come visiting with their checkbooks. But come, sit down, and let's have a chat to catch up."

She led me to a light-blue leather couch next to the window overlooking the Charles River and sat across from me in a matching wingback chair. As we sat down, the receptionist came in with mugs of coffee and a small basket of scones.

"Still take it black?"

I smiled and took one of the coffees. "Still black. I'm surprised you remember. It's been nearly two years."

"Yes, but we went through a pretty intense time together. Things stick. How's Karen doing?"

"She's good. She's with the FBI now, you know."

"And the two of you are still together? Happy? I always saw myself as a bit of a matchmaker, even if it was inadvertent."

I laughed. True, she'd introduced us when she directed me to work with Karen on the Singer case. But I wasn't sure that qualified as being a matchmaker.

"Karen and I are living together now, and we're doing great. But I'm not sure that introducing us by forcing us to work together gives you matchmaker status. As I remember, you were actually pretty ticked off when we first became romantically involved."

She gave me a playful wink. "Only because it screwed up my investigation. And anyway, all's well that ends well."

"Fair enough. As president, you're entitled to claim whatever secondary title you please. How do you like running the university?"

I was beginning to wonder what this meeting was about. She couldn't really have time to have brought me here simply for a reunion chat.

"I'm not sure I ever get enough time to think about how I like it. It's insanely busy, mostly with fundraising. There are some rewarding aspects, but also some tough decisions. Especially when it comes to personnel. When I was dean, I always thought dealing with tenure cases was the hardest thing I had to do. The responsibility of recommending whether or not a young faculty member would keep their job or get kicked out on their ass weighed on me. But now the weight of that decision is much greater. As dean, I just made a recommendation. As president, I have the final say in making or breaking someone's career."

"I can imagine. Tenure was always the toughest thing for me to deal with when I was department chair. It tore me up when I had to make a negative recommendation. Sometimes it was clearly the right thing to do, but other times it could just be that they hadn't published in quite the right journals or hadn't gotten invited to enough of the top conferences. In cases like that, it just didn't seem fair. I'm glad to be out of that now."

She nodded sympathetically. "Yes, I can understand why you feel that way. Unfortunately, I've asked you here because I need you to get back into a leadership position. If only for a short while."

So that's why I was here. Another leadership position. What the hell did that mean? Department chair again? Or something worse, like being a dean. Whatever it was, I had to get out of it. I'd done my time.

I took a scone to pause the conversation before answering. I couldn't just refuse a direct request from the president of the university. But maybe I could wriggle my way out of it.

"I'm sorry. You know I'd like to help if I could. But I'm just getting my lab going again after being away for a year on sabbatical. Our research is finally off the ground, and we've reached a critical stage where I need to recruit new students and build momentum. There's no way I can afford to take on an administrative role now."

Her face hardened as she sat up straight in her chair. "I understand, but I wouldn't ask you to do this if it wasn't important. Yes, it'll take some of your time, but it won't be for long. And I'm quite sure you'll be able to continue your research. BTI needs your help, Brad, and I want you to hear me out."

The look on her face left no question that I was talking to President Houghton, not chatting with an old friend.

"Of course. I apologize if I sounded too negative at first." What else could I say?

"Good, thank you. What do you know about MTRI, the Maine Translational Research Institute?"

"Not much. I know that BTI is involved in some sort of satellite operation in Maine, but I haven't paid much attention to it."

"Yes, I've gotten the idea that you'd rather ignore university politics. Anyway, you're correct. MTRI's been in operation for about four years now. It's staffed by twenty or so principal investigators, all of whom hold faculty positions at BTI."

"Why set up an operation like that in Maine instead of here? It has to be tough to operate a satellite research facility from a distance."

She took a sip of coffee. "It is, but there seems to be a need. Maine has a big cancer problem, with an incidence substantially higher than the national average. Lung cancer, of course, is the biggest offender. The focus of MTRI is experimental cancer treatment, and we hope it provides Mainers with some additional options for taking advantage of the latest advances. As well as giving our faculty members a chance to recruit a new patient population for clinical trials."

"Got it. So the advantage for us is that a satellite facility up there can recruit patients without having to directly compete with all the other places in Boston."

"Right, while at the same time, offering patients from Maine access to all the trials that are going on at the Boston hospitals we're affiliated with."

"Okay, sounds like a good deal for both Maine and BTI. Where's it located?"

"We wanted it to be close enough to Boston that going back and forth would be easy, as well as serving a part of the state that wasn't right on top of the Maine Medical Center in Portland. We found a spot on the southern coast in Wells. It's only about ninety minutes from here."

"And what's the problem? Isn't it working out?"

She sighed. "I have a director who's resigned in the middle of an especially messy tenure controversy. There are two assistant professors coming up for tenure at the same time, and one of them is claiming some of the senior faculty are biased against her. Worse than that, she's suggested that her research may have been sabotaged by the other candidate. The director of the institute doesn't buy into her accusations, and the whole place seems embroiled in this ugly tenure fight. In the meantime, the director resigned his position two weeks ago. He had a standing offer from Princeton, and I think he basically decided that he didn't need to hassle with this kind of crap."

I rolled my eyes. "Please tell me that you're not asking me to step in as director in the middle of this mess. True, cancer research is my field—but I'm a basic scientist, not a clinician."

"Just on a temporary basis, as acting director. I'm already talking to a good candidate for the position, but she can't come for another six months. And I'm aware that you're not a physician, but you know enough about cancer treatment to manage things as a stopgap. What we really need is someone who can handle the personnel crisis—which is what you're good at."

"But I can't just pick up and move to Maine for six months. It'll set my lab back to square one. Not to mention leaving Karen."

"You wouldn't have to be there full-time. Remember, it's only ninety minutes away. We'd set you up with a house in Wells, and you could arrange to spend maybe two or three days a week there. And I'm sure Karen would enjoy spending some time up there, too. I understand it's a nice place in the summer."

She had it all planned out. And it was hard—if not impossible—to refuse a direct request from the president of the university. I made one last objection, even though I knew it wouldn't hold.

"I don't know. Being away from the lab for even a few days a week is a problem. The students working with me are still new, they need daily guidance."

"Would it help if I provided funding for a senior research associate to supervise the lab while you're away? The kind of support we provided when you were department chair. I'm happy to do anything I can to make this work for you."

I sighed inwardly. That didn't leave me much of an out. "Yes, that would certainly help maintain continuity in the lab. I appreciate it."

She smiled. "Good. And housing? Maybe a place on the beach? MTRI's only a couple of miles inland from the coast."

This was getting tempting, at least since it was clear that I couldn't say no. Karen and I had enjoyed visiting Wells Beach last summer, before we got embroiled in the nightmare of Walter Monroe. A couple of days a week there, with visits from Karen, wouldn't be a bad thing. Especially since I didn't have any choice.

I inclined my head in a gesture of acceptance. "As long as dogs are allowed. We won't want to leave Rosie at home."

Claire Houghton rolled her eyes. "Rosie's your pug, isn't she? Okay, dog-friendly it'll be."

3

I brought both candidates' files home that evening. They'd been waiting for me when I left President Houghton's office, a symbolic reminder that I never really had any choice about accepting my new assignment.

The walk home still felt a bit odd to me. Karen and I had bought the house in Brookline together a little over six months ago. Neither her old condo in the North End nor mine in Back Bay was big enough for both of us, and it had gotten to the point where shuttling back and forth between the two places was a substantial nuisance. We'd finally taken the leap and sold them both to buy a newly renovated three-bedroom colonial, which gave each of us an office and all the room we needed to officially live together. It was on a tree-lined street that was close to the city, but not in the middle of it, so it had a pleasantly suburban feeling. There was even a deck and a backyard, which we promptly fenced in so that Rosie could have a place of her own. And like my old place, it was just over a mile from my lab at BTI. I just had to remember to head west instead of east on Commonwealth Avenue when I left the office.

This evening, I was sufficiently preoccupied with the MTRI tenure cases that I turned the wrong way when I started home, proceeding east on Commonwealth in the direction of my old condo. I'd gone a couple of blocks before I caught myself and turned around. It didn't matter; there was no particular rush. I'd be home by six, and Karen was planning to leave work early to relax and cook dinner, which I figured would provide a quiet evening to tell her about my new job.

Except when I got home, Karen was nowhere to be found. Instead, I was greeted by an excited Rosie who was equally eager for affection, a treat, and a chance to go out. I picked her up for a cuddle, gave her a piece of her favorite chicken jerky, and followed her out to the deck, where I sat in one of the lounge chairs while she ran around sniffing until she was satisfied that everything was in order. At which point she relieved herself, ran back to the deck, and jumped up in my lap.

So where was Karen? I couldn't help feeling a twinge of worry. Being an FBI agent wasn't exactly a hazard-free occupation. But she hadn't said that anything in particular was planned for today, and it wasn't unusual for her to be late. Sometimes things came up unexpectedly. And it was only a few minutes after six, not that late. Except that she'd been planning to come home early.

Just as I was thinking that a text would have been nice, my phone buzzed.

Sorry, some unplanned crap hit. Don't worry, I'm fine. Home in an hour or so. I'll tell you about it then. And I'll still handle dinner!

I smiled as I read it. She must have read my mind, which was something she seemed to have a way of doing. But if she was still thinking about dinner, whatever had happened couldn't be all that bad. Although in Karen's world, "not that bad" could include some pretty violent crimes.

A light rain started to fall, so I went in and gave Rosie her dinner. Then I poured myself a glass of scotch and settled into my usual chair in the living room—Karen called it my Archie Bunker chair—with the tenure files. I'd gone through them during the day, but I'd had other distractions. An hour before Karen got home would give me time for an uninterrupted second look.

I started with Mark Heller. There was no question about his case—he'd been a golden boy from day one. He'd obtained both an MD and a PhD in cancer biology from Harvard, followed by three years of clinical research at Stanford. He had publications in top journals from both Harvard and Stanford, which had gotten him a position as an assistant professor at BTI six years ago. He'd then spearheaded the development of a new drug—aloxinor—that was targeted against one of the genes frequently involved in lung cancers. Heller had not only done the lab work on aloxinor, but he'd then shepherded the drug through a successful clinical trial. It was now an approved treatment that promised to extend the lives of many lung cancer patients, although there was still the problem that it was only effective for a few months. After that, cancers that had initially responded became resistant and patients relapsed. His research was now concentrated on finding ways to overcome that problematic drug resistance, and he'd jumped at the chance to recruit an expanded patient population by moving to MTRI three years ago.

His record of publication in top journals had continued unabated during his years as an assistant professor, he was a frequent speaker at prestigious national and international meetings, and he'd achieved a high level of funding for his research, with both federal grants and pharmaceutical company support. Perhaps most important for a successful tenure case, twelve leaders in his field from other universities—Yale, Princeton, Harvard, Berkeley, and the like—all evaluated his accomplishments in glowing terms and stated unequivocally that he would receive tenure at their institutions.

A case couldn't get any stronger. The only hitch was that the second candidate, Carolyn Gelman, had accused Heller of sabotaging her research. An accusation which, if true, could very well lead to his dismissal, rather than promotion to the coveted permanent position of tenured professor.

Gelman also had a strong record, but notably less spectacular than Heller's. Her degrees were from Yale, followed by residency and postdoctoral research at the University of Wisconsin. As an assistant professor, she'd concentrated on combination drug therapies, in part as a way of overcoming the problem of drug resistance. Her lab was well funded, and she had several strong publications, although only two in truly top journals. None of the drug combinations she'd developed had gained FDA approval, but one was now in clinical trial. Most of the outside letters were supportive, but three of the ten noted that they'd never met her because she seldom went to meetings or gave seminars at other institutions. Consequently, although she appeared to do good work, they weren't sure that she had established herself as a leader in her field or that she was well enough known to get tenure at their institutions.

Those negatives were serious, but I didn't think they were lethal in themselves. Overall, Gelman had a strong record of productivity, and the majority of outside evaluators supported her case. I also noted that she had two small children, which could be why she didn't travel as much to meetings as she might otherwise have done.

But that still left the problem that her case would be directly compared to Heller's. They were both coming up for tenure at the same time from the same small satellite institution, and there was no way that the university committee responsible for evaluating tenure cases could avoid comparing them side by side. And in that comparison, Gelman would come out a weak second. It would take a strong advocate to get her successfully through the tenure process.

Was that why Claire Houghton had asked me to step in? But Gelman had now complicated the situation further by her accusations of bias and sabotage. A critical freezer in her lab had been unplugged a couple of weeks ago, and she blamed Heller for it. It was a shocking allegation, and everything would hinge on whether or not she was believed. Getting to the bottom of her story was clearly my top priority.

I was starting to contemplate my first moves when Rosie jumped off my lap and ran to the door. She'd sensed someone approaching the house; Karen must be home. I made a quick stop in the kitchen to pour a glass of Sauvignon Blanc and got to the door just as Karen came in. Which meant that Rosie jumped on her and I kissed her pretty much simultaneously.

"You two certainly know how to make a girl feel welcome," she laughed. "Is that wine for me, too?"

"It is, and you are. Welcome, that is. But you look a bit worn. What went on to hold you up this afternoon?"

"Let's sit down and I'll fill you in. And I want to hear about your meeting with BTI's new president." She took my hand and led me back to the living room, where she sat on the couch and patted the seat next to her. Rosie, of course, thought that was her signal to jump up, so I had to squeeze in beside the two of them.

"Everything was calm until around four, when I was getting ready to leave," Karen said. "Then we got a call about a shooting at the Harbor Inn in Revere. I guess you haven't been watching the news?"

"No, I've been reading work stuff."

She nodded. "Got it. Anyway, three bodies were found in a room, all shot in the head at close range. Turns out the victims were Russian mobsters involved in a major drug operation."

"You're assuming it was a gang hit then?"

"That's what we think. ME put the time of death around midnight last night. The room was registered to one of the victims, who was due to check out today. When he wasn't heard from, the manager investigated."

"Any clues?"

"Not really. There's CCTV coverage of the hallway, which shows someone knocking on the door and entering the room just after twelve o'clock. Then the same person leaves a few minutes later. His face is hidden both times, so no way we can make an ID."

"Sounds like the victims knew the killer if they let him in, right?"

"That's what we think. Our agents have been watching the guys who were shot for several months now and think they've been skimming cash off the top. The Russians are notorious for not tolerating that kind of thing, so our bet is that the killer was a mob enforcer who set up a meet. When they let him in, he did his work."

"Any chance of getting him?"

"I doubt it. He's obviously a pro to finish off three victims like that. Otherwise, we don't have a clue. He'll be long gone by now."

She took a drink of wine. "So that was my day at the office. Now I'm ready to hear about something else. Like your meeting with President Houghton."

"It didn't have the excitement of your day, although I do have some unexpected news. But should we do something about dinner first? Maybe go out?"

"Nope, it's all set. I told you I'd take care of dinner tonight." She checked her watch. "It'll be here in half an hour."

"Should I ask how you managed that?"

"Sushi, with all the ones you like best. I had plenty of time to place an order while we were waiting for news to come in from the scene."

I inclined my head and gave her a mock salute. "Okay, then. On to my meeting?"

She nodded. "I assume it was calmer than our last visit to the Presidential Palace."

I had to chuckle at that. "When you arrested Emerson and we hauled him out in handcuffs? Yes, it was definitely calmer than that. Though a bit of a surprise."

She listened while I filled her in on Claire Houghton's request, taking occasional sips of wine but not interrupting until I finished. Then she gave me a wry smile.

"I assume you're going to do it. It's not like you really have a choice anyway, right?"

I shrugged. "It wouldn't be easy to turn her down, but there's always a choice. It'd be pretty disruptive, not just for my research, but also for us. How do you feel about it?"

Before she could answer, Rosie jumped up and raced to the door. Dinner had arrived.

By the time I'd paid the deliveryman, Karen had moved our drinks to the dining table and was putting out dinner plates with little dishes for soy sauce and wasabi. I started taking the sushi out of the bag while she went back to the kitchen and returned with a bottle of soy sauce from the fridge. She didn't like dealing with the little packages the restaurant provided.

"That's quite a spread you got us," I said, when we had everything arranged.

She smiled. "I even got a couple pieces of your favorite. Octopus."

"So I see. But I thought you didn't like them."

"I don't, they're all yours. But I made up for it and got some of the egg sushi for myself."

I clinked her wine glass with my scotch. "Fair enough, I can't stand those. But everything else looks great." I added wasabi to my soy sauce and took a piece of tuna maki to start. "So back to the idea of my being acting director of this place in Maine. What do you think?"

"We can live with it if we have to. It's temporary and it sounds like you'll only need to be there a couple of days a week. And who could complain about a place on the beach in Wells for the summer? I'll come visit whenever I can, maybe even manage a bit of a vacation. But how about the effect on your research? Can you handle that?"

"Like you said at first, I don't have a lot of choice. The lab'll survive, and the president said she'd give me a senior research associate to help manage when I'm away."

"Okay then, sounds like we're in. So tell me, what do you think about the claim the woman's making about her work being sabotaged? Her name's Carolyn, right?"

"Yes, Carolyn Gelman. And those claims are the heart of the matter. She's said that her competitor, Mark Heller, has criticized her work to students and colleagues, making it hard for her to even run her lab. And, more drastic, that he unplugged her freezer intending to destroy critical research material."

"Criticizing her work seems a little hard to pin down. After all, scientists are allowed to say what they want, right? But unplugging a freezer? You said he's a much stronger candidate, so why would he do something like that? It seems stupid."

"You're right. His tenure case couldn't be stronger; he doesn't need to sabotage hers. And if he was really guilty of doing something like that, it'd be the end of his career. It doesn't make sense for him to risk it."

"But someone did it. Could Heller be more worried about the tenure business than you think he should be?"

"No question that it was intentional sabotage. Not only was the freezer unplugged, but the alarm was turned off and the door was left open. If a student in a neighboring lab hadn't caught it in time, it would have destroyed the blood samples from Gelman's clinical trial and set her research back for months. But that doesn't mean it was Heller."

"Did someone check the freezer for prints?"

"Yes, they called in the local cops. The only prints belonged to Gelman and two of her students."

"But of course, Heller—or someone else—could have worn gloves. Are there other suspects?"

I shrugged. "Nobody in particular, but it could be anyone with a grudge against her. Or for that matter, against one of her students or postdocs who had material in the freezer. Something similar happened to me a few years ago, and it turned out to be a disgruntled graduate student who'd failed her qualifying exam. I'd been on the committee and she blamed me for it."

"Doesn't sound like it'll be simple to sort out. How are you going to get to the bottom of it?"

I took the last piece of sushi. The second octopus nigiri, which I'd been saving. The best for last.

"I'll start by going up to MTRI two weeks from now, on what will be the current director's last day. I'll talk to him before he fades away, and then start meeting some of the faculty members. Including our two tenure candidates."

"That'll give you a sense of the players. Then what?"

"Can't tell you that yet. I guess I'll just poke around until I get some insight into what's happening." I gave her a playful grin. "Sort of the way you handle your investigations, right?"

She raised her glass with a smile. "Sounds like detective work to me."

4

I spent the next several days talking to my students and postdocs about my new schedule and planning out their experiments far enough in advance that my absences wouldn't be a problem. I promised to be back at least a couple of days a week and to be available by email or Zoom while I was away. They'd be fine. Or so I hoped.

I also sent an email to Janet Klein, who'd worked with me as a senior research associate to help run my lab when I'd been department chair. She'd since taken a job with a biotech startup, but I knew she wasn't happy with the corporate environment. So I took a chance and asked if she might just possibly be interested in coming back, adding that I had funding for her on a long-term basis, beyond the end of my tenure at MTRI. Her response was immediate and enthusiastic—she'd be thrilled to be back at BTI.

With that stroke of luck, I felt reasonably confident when I headed off to MTRI. The lab would survive a period of my divided attention, especially with Janet's help. Now I just had a messy tenure case to sort out. Nothing I hadn't done before.

The rain fell steadily, making the traffic getting out of Boston even worse than usual. It didn't let up until I left Massachusetts behind and crossed into New Hampshire, at which point the traffic thinned and I made up for lost time on the final stretch north on I-95 into southern Maine. I got off at the Wells exit, from which it was less than two miles to College Drive. A short stretch through mostly open wooded land then led to York Community College and, a little farther down, MTRI.

The building was not what I expected. Rather than sleek glass and steel construction, like contemporary lab buildings in Boston, MTRI was housed in a redbrick building that looked like it belonged to an older era. The style was similar to the York Community College buildings and was a much better fit to the open wooded area than more modern-looking construction would have been. I guessed that it also provided a homier setting for cancer patients wanting to explore their treatment options.

I walked up a landscaped path from the parking lot to the front entrance, which was flanked by two climbing mandevilla vines. A hummingbird hovered over their fragrant pink flowers as if it had the job of welcoming visitors.

There was a building directory just inside, so I stopped to take in the layout. The institute's administrative offices and patient care facilities—including waiting areas, rooms for exams and consultations, a pharmacy, and clinical laboratories—were located on the first two floors. The upper five floors housed faculty offices and research laboratories.

I proceeded through a set of glass doors leading to the administrative office suite, where I was greeted by a studious-looking young woman seated at an oak reception desk. I identified myself and said I had an appointment with Director Lowell.

"Oh, you're our new director! I'm so happy to meet you. I'm Anna, let me take you right in."

She led me to a door behind her desk and knocked softly. It was opened by a heavy-set man with a balding head of gray hair. "Brad Parker, I presume? I'm Dan Lowell. Pleasure to meet you."

I shook his hand as I looked around the office, which was mostly packed up and filled with moving boxes.

"Sorry about the mess. I'll have this all cleaned out for you shortly," he said. "Movers are coming this afternoon, and Anna can help you get settled in tomorrow morning. But I suspect you want to chat a bit first."

"Yes, I'd appreciate that." I took a seat at a six-person conference table toward the front of the room. Lowell sat across from me, and I said, "Anything you want to tell me in terms of an entry debriefing would be most welcome."

"I think you'll find the overall operations and budget pretty straightforward. And I have an excellent associate director, who's thoroughly briefed and handles the routine kind of stuff. Jim Putnam. Keep him on and you shouldn't have any problems."

"Great; having someone like that is an enormous help. I understand there's a somewhat acute problem that needs attention, though."

He sighed. "The tenure cases. Yes, I'm afraid so. Goddamned mess, to tell you the truth."

"So I've gathered. I've read both candidates' files, but I'd be grateful for your take on the situation."

"Sure. One of them, Mark Heller, is a no-brainer. The guy's done everything right and the case is rock-solid, with full support from the senior faculty. Carolyn Gelman's case, on the other hand, is borderline, and some of our influential faculty don't like her. You probably also know that she's made accusations to the effect that she's been unfairly treated, even that Mark has sabotaged her work."

"I'm aware."

"Well, those kinds of complaints haven't made her any more popular with her colleagues. It's hard for me to see where her case has a positive outcome. I've tried to counsel her about looking for another job and leaving before she's kicked out, but there's no way she'll listen."

"I'm surprised you've tried to counsel her out. The case doesn't seem that bad to me. Not as strong as Heller's, sure. But on her own merits, I'd consider her well above the bar for tenure. Well funded, good publications, an important clinical trial in progress. A clear majority of outside letters are positive, and the couple of negatives just complain that she doesn't go to enough meetings."

He looked at me with a raised eyebrow. "But when her case is compared to Mark's? I don't see how it'll fly."

That was indeed the crux of the problem, but I didn't like the way he approached it. He sounded smug.

"I understand your concern, but each candidate for tenure is supposed to be evaluated individually—not compared to others. There's no reason why she and Heller shouldn't both be granted tenure if their records merit it. Which I think they do, at least from what I've seen in the files."

"I'm sure she'll be glad that her new director feels that way. But I'm afraid you'll find yourself at odds with several of the senior faculty here. I suspect the addition of their views to the file will put the nail in the coffin."

"All right, tell me: What's her problem with those faculty?"

"Basically, she's a bitch. A nasty woman who thinks she's better than everyone else and doesn't want to do the yeoman's work needed to keep the place running."

It was obvious that Lowell was one of the faculty members opposed to tenure. No wonder she hadn't been interested in his advice about looking for another job.

"Can you give me some specifics? Just saying that she's a bitch doesn't help me much."

He grunted his displeasure. "No, I suppose not. Well, if I try to step back a bit, I guess the big problem is her attitude. She's self-centered and refuses to spend time on anything that doesn't directly forward her own research."

If that were true, it was indeed the kind of attitude that would get her into trouble. Any academic department was a community, in which faculty members had to do their share of the mundane tasks needed to keep things running. On the other hand, when I was a department chair, I'd always tried to protect junior faculty from routine chores so that they could focus on their research.

I needed more information, but Lowell already looked defensive. Pushing him too hard would be counterproductive.

"Okay, I see where an attitude like that would cause problems for her. What sort of things did she refuse to do?"

"Like I said, anything that didn't help her research. As you know, there's lots of maintenance work and faculty committees needed to run an institute. Library committee, seminar committee, thesis committees for students, search committees for new faculty. Whenever she was asked to participate in something like that, she'd just say that she couldn't do it. No real excuses, just that she didn't have the time."

I rolled my eyes. "I'm sure her colleagues didn't appreciate that."

"Exactly. It was like she thought she was better than everyone else and shouldn't have to do her share. Not only that, she insists on leaving promptly at four thirty every afternoon. She won't stay later than that for meetings, seminars, taking visitors out to dinner. Lots of things happen in the late afternoon or evening, but she'd just fade away."

"I noticed that she has two young children. Is it a child-care problem?"

Lowell shrugged. "Maybe, but lots of young women have kids and still manage to fulfill their professional obligations. Her husband's a big-shot lawyer with a firm in Portland. Plenty of money, a big house on the beach. She could afford to get help with child care."

I knew it wasn't always that simple, but there was nothing to gain from arguing with him. He'd be gone tomorrow. Instead, I decided to move the conversation on to the next issue I needed to probe.

"Okay, I can understand where she's gotten some of her colleagues annoyed at her. Which certainly hasn't been very smart on her part, although I don't think it constitutes appropriate grounds for denying tenure. But she's also claimed that some of the MTRI faculty have bad-mouthed her and even attempted to sabotage her work. What are your thoughts on that?"

"I assume you know that she's leveled those accusations specifically against Mark Heller. Her argument is that he's trying to take her down to advance his own tenure case."

I nodded. "And what do you think?"

"Why the hell would he do that, when she's obviously no competition? Maybe he's said some things that are critical of her work, I don't know. I'm sure other faculty members have, too. Talking about each other's work is something that scientists do all the time. It's not like there's some kind of conspiracy against her."

His dismissiveness annoyed me. "How about her freezer having been unplugged? Does that happen all the time, too?"

He frowned and looked down at the table. "No, that really does seem to have been an intentional act of sabotage. But again, blaming Mark for it has pissed people off rather than getting any sympathy for her."

"I assume you've investigated. Do you have any idea of what happened?"

"We can reconstruct some of it. A student in another lab went into the common equipment room and noticed that the freezer was unplugged and its door was ajar. That was about two in the morning. He called Gelman, and she told him to plug it back in and close the door. Then she came into the lab herself to check. That was when she noticed the emergency alarm had been turned off. The temperature had only risen about twenty degrees at that point, so fortunately nothing was thawed."

"The fact that the emergency alarm was turned off obviously means it wasn't an accident," I said.

He nodded. "Obviously. And from the temperature rise, we're guessing that it probably happened between twelve thirty and one o'clock."

"I don't suppose there's any way of knowing who was in the building then?"

"Not really. But there's a security camera on the front door, so we know who goes in and out. And we probably have a picture of the guilty party doing just that."

I sat up straight in my chair. This was something new.

"And? Can you identify them?"

"Unfortunately not. Here, I'll show you."

He got up and I followed him over to his desk. He clicked the mouse on his computer and said, "I can access the security video from here. Watch."

The video started at midnight the night of the incident. Lowell fast-forwarded to twelve fifteen. Then he slowed it and we watched someone enter the building. The face was completely covered by the hood of a black parka. Lowell fast-forwarded again to twenty minutes later, when the same figure left. Still completely shielded by the hood.

"You're assuming that's who it was because of the time? Seems reasonable enough," I said.

"The cops thought so, too. But who it is remains a mystery."

"So the cops reviewed the tape as well as checking the freezer? I saw in the file that the only prints they found on the freezer belonged to Gelman and members of her lab."

"Correct. They couldn't tell much more from the tape, either."

"There's nothing that rules Heller out. He could have worn gloves, so the absence of prints doesn't mean much."

"No, the tape doesn't rule Mark out. But there's another potential suspect who's a better fit."

"Who's that?"

He looked up at me with a nasty grin. "Carolyn Gelman. A lot of us think she sabotaged her own freezer to gain sympathy and put the blame on Mark."

5

I was pensive when I left Lowell's office. I had a clear picture of how Gelman had earned the resentment of some of her colleagues. And she'd be understandably nervous about coming up for tenure under those conditions, especially at the same time as a powerhouse like Heller. But had she really unplugged her own freezer? It was possible, and Lowell seemed nearly convinced. I didn't like him, but that didn't mean he was wrong.

Anna interrupted my speculation as I passed the reception desk. "Dr. Parker? You might be interested in this. It's Dr. Gelman's tenure seminar."

She handed me an announcement of a seminar at two o'clock that afternoon. Dr. Carolyn Gelman, speaking about "Combination Chemotherapy to Treat Drug-Resistant Cancers."

Gelman's tenure seminar was something I most certainly wanted to hear. So why hadn't Lowell brought it to my attention? Jerk.

"It'll be in the seventh-floor seminar room," Anna said. "Shall I tell Dr. Lowell that you'll be going? It would be a good chance for him to introduce you to the faculty."

"Thanks, Anna, I appreciate your bringing this to my attention. I'll definitely go, but no need to bother Dr. Lowell. I don't want to be a distraction, so I'll just sneak in and sit in the back. There'll be plenty of time for me to meet the faculty later."

***

I got to the seminar room a few minutes after two and took a seat in the back row. It looked like about two-thirds of what I guessed to be around fifty seats were occupied. Lowell was at the podium, just starting his introduction of the speaker, so my entrance was unnoticed.

The introductions of speakers at tenure seminars were usually somewhat flashy. This was the candidate's opportunity to impress the faculty who would be voting on their promotion, and whoever was introducing the candidate normally took the time to review their career and highlight their accomplishments in glowing terms. In other words, to help them put their best foot forward.

Lowell was having none of that. He summarily noted that Gelman had received MD and PhD degrees from Yale, had done postgraduate work at the University of Wisconsin, and then joined BTI as an assistant professor. She'd come to MTRI three years ago and was now a candidate for tenure. Her work focused on combination chemotherapy for drug-resistant cancers, which she'd be talking about today.

With that he stepped away from the podium, with no welcoming applause from either him or the audience. It was a cold introduction for a tenure candidate he obviously couldn't care less about.

Despite the chill in the room, Gelman looked calm and confident as she strode to the podium. A tall woman with shoulder-length black hair, she was dressed professionally in a light-gray jacket, cream-colored blouse, and dark-gray slacks. Ignoring the obvious hostility, she thanked Lowell for his very kind introduction and the audience for coming to her talk. Then she launched smoothly into a description of her research, using a PowerPoint presentation on her laptop via a ceiling-mounted LCD projector.

She gave a good talk. She was a bit too rigid and formal, without any attempt at humor to engage the audience—but what else could she do, given the unmistakable air of hostility in the room? She started by reviewing the development of gene-targeted therapies and presented data from a number of studies showing their initial effectiveness, all too often followed by failure when cancers inevitably became resistant to the drugs. Then she focused on drugs that acted by inhibiting a class of enzymes called receptor tyrosine kinases, or RTKs. These were the most common anti-cancer drugs, which included Mark Heller's aloxinor. As was the case for most RTK inhibitors, a high percentage of patients responded to aloxinor, but those responses typically lasted only a few months before the development of resistance led to relapse.

Gelman then went on to explain that drug resistance could occur in a variety of different ways. Sometimes the RTK targeted by the drug mutated, making the drug no longer effective. One approach to dealing with this kind of drug resistance was to develop modified drugs that worked on the mutated target. This was sometimes successful and was, in fact, the approach that Heller was pursuing to fight resistance to aloxinor.

However, Gelman was hoping to develop a more general strategy. Most RTKs converged on a small number of downstream targets within cancer cells. With that in mind, she had decided to approach the problem by combining inhibitors of these downstream targets with RTK inhibitors. Her hope was that inhibition of downstream targets would prevent development of resistance to the whole group of drugs that worked by RTK inhibition, not just to any one agent.

It seemed like a plausible but chancy approach. It could pay off big, but it could just as easily flop. I wasn't at all sure that it was a direction I myself would choose to try. Especially not before I had the job security that only came with tenure.

However, the data she proceeded to show were impressive. Using aloxinor and one other common RTK inhibitor—retoramib—as models, she first tested the effectiveness of downstream inhibitors in preventing the development of resistance in cancer cells grown in culture dishes. The results were clear-cut: Her basic strategy worked, at least for cells outside the body.

Studies in mice came next, and she showed the audience results that were really striking. A low, nontoxic dose of downstream inhibitors substantially interfered with the development of drug resistance in cancers in mice. Obviously not the perfect model for human cancers—there were many cancer treatments that looked promising in mice, but failed when they were tried in the clinic. But the results she had were certainly encouraging.

And she wasn't done yet. She went on to discuss the clinical trial that was now in progress. It was early days, but she already had some intriguing results to show. She'd established a nontoxic dose of downstream inhibitors, similar to the nontoxic dose in mice. Then she'd combined this with aloxinor and retoramib treatments. And at least early indications were that her protocol significantly delayed the emergence of resistant cancers. She concluded by appropriately acknowledging that these results, while encouraging, were still preliminary and the trial was continuing.

It was an impressive talk, and I expected it to be followed by a round of enthusiastic applause. But not so. I was one of less than half the audience who clapped their hands, and most of the others who applauded at all made only perfunctory offerings. It had to be disappointing, even insulting, for the speaker. But Gelman maintained her rigid professionalism and said she would be happy to answer any questions.

Only a few people raised their hands, and several got up to leave, purposely showing their lack of interest. Gelman pretended not to notice, instead calling on a man with his hand raised in the second row.

"Yes, Mark?"

So that was presumably Mark Heller. I was curious—would he be deliberately hostile?

"Very nice talk, Carolyn. Your data look quite good. I was wondering, though, why you've chosen aloxinor for your clinical trial. As you know, my colleagues and I developed aloxinor relatively recently, and we're also investigating approaches to overcome resistance. So I'm curious why you didn't choose to work with any of the several other RTK inhibitors where more is known about resistance mechanisms."

Heller's question was framed politely, but clearly designed to remind everyone that aloxinor was *his* drug. With the thinly veiled implication that Gelman was poaching on his territory.

Gelman kept her cool. "We chose aloxinor because—to your credit, Mark—it's one of the most effective drugs currently available. But resistance is still a problem, so we thought it would be an impactful example of us to start with. Of course, we're testing our approach with another RTK inhibitor, retoramib, at the same time."

It was a good answer, but apparently not enough to satisfy a woman seated in the row behind Heller. She waved her hand, and Gelman recognized her. She didn't mince words.

"Aloxinor seems like an odd choice to me, Dr. Gelman. As you're well aware, it was developed by Dr. Heller, our colleague. Although he may be too polite to say so, it seems to me that you're stepping on his toes by choosing to work on it. Especially since some of his own current work concerns drug resistance as well."

I stared at the back of the woman's head in surprise. She was out of line, her hostility abundantly clear. Gelman just stood there blinking for a moment. When she finally spoke, she managed it well.

"I'm sorry you feel that way, Dr. Osborne, but I assure you that I'm in no way attempting to infringe on Mark's work. There's no dispute that aloxinor is his drug, and as I just said, it's an excellent one. That's why we're trying to make it still better. As is Mark. We have a common goal here—beating cancer."

Before Osborne could say anything else, Gelman recognized a white-haired man with his hand raised in the back of the room. "Dr. Carlson?"

"Dr. Gelman, leaving aside the dubious ethics of your choosing to work on aloxinor, my question concerns the reproducibility and reliability of your results. You've shown us what would appear to be promising clinical data, but it seems very preliminary. Are there any confirmations of your observations? Otherwise, I would suggest that much of what you presented should be taken with a grain of salt, not viewed as serious science."

That was so insulting and inappropriate that I started to stand up to say something in Gelman's defense. It was obvious that Carlson was simply out to embarrass her, with no intention of giving her a fair chance. But before I could say anything, Gelman lashed out.

"You're full of crap! My data are completely reliable, and I clearly pointed out that the clinical trial is still a work in progress. You're just trying to throw up a smokescreen of bullshit to block my promotion. I can only hope that our colleagues are too smart to listen to you."

With that she turned and stomped out, using a door behind the podium to make an angry exit.

I kept my seat as the audience filed out. At least some of them seemed to have the good sense to look embarrassed. Maybe even contrite.

Not Carlson. It took some effort to contain myself when he walked past me, a self-satisfied look in his eyes. But now wasn't the time to give him the chewing out he deserved. That would have to wait for the privacy of my office tomorrow morning.

6

The house that had been rented for me wouldn't be ready for move-in until Friday—tomorrow afternoon—so I spent the night at the Old Village Inn in Ogunquit. The inn dated to the mid-nineteenth century and my room possessed the charm of that era, with a four-poster bed and an ocean-view balcony. The dining room was equally pleasant and featured an extensive selection of single malts—including my favorite, Oban. I celebrated my new job with a glass of scotch and an excellent grilled breast of duck. I was tempted by the baked stuffed lobster, but decided to save that for dinner tomorrow night with Karen, when she came up for the weekend.

I took a walk down to the beach after dinner and then called Karen to check in on the day's events. She seemed most interested in the fact that there was a security video of someone entering the institute at the time the freezer was sabotaged. If I sent it to her, she suggested, perhaps her folks at the Bureau could come up with some notion of the intruder's general appearance.

When I got to MTRI the next morning, Anna showed me into what was now my new director's office. Bare and empty, except for the desk, conference table, and assorted chairs. Lowell had been good to his word—boxes and everything else was gone. The only thing left on the desk was a phone.

"We have a new computer and printer for you," Anna said. "I'll have IT come set them up whenever you're ready. And I have an assortment of desk supplies in a closet in the outer office. Maybe you can take a look and let me know what you need. Or what else I should order for you. Is there anything else you'd like me to get? I could bring in some plants, or maybe get some pictures to hang on the walls. You could use something in here to make it feel a bit more homey."

I looked around at the bare walls. "I guess it could use some decorating, but I didn't bring anything. Not my first priority. Why don't you have IT come and set up the computer, and while they're doing that, you can bring me an assortment of desk supplies. Whatever you choose will be fine. And then I'd like to see Tom Carlson."

"Will do. When do you want me to try and get Dr. Carlson to come in? He keeps a pretty busy schedule, so he can be hard to get hold of."

"I want him here as soon as IT's finished. Let's say an hour. And you can tell him I don't give a damn about his schedule."

She smiled. "You got it, boss."

Maybe I wasn't the only one who thought Carlson was a pig.

* * *

The IT guy was quick—it took less than half an hour to get my new computer set up and running. When he finished, I asked him to show me how to access the security camera recordings. He seemed surprised by the request, but dutifully pulled up the link. Once he left, I emailed the recording of the illicit entry to Karen. Then I began refreshing my memory of Carlson's CV until Anna knocked on the door.

"He's here; shall I show him in?"

I looked at my watch. He was five minutes late. "No, let him sit and stew for a bit. Give it ten minutes, then you can bring him."

There was no denying that Carlson had an impressive record. Now in his mid-sixties, some fifteen years my senior, he could claim responsibility for the development of nearly half a dozen useful drugs. He was a member of several prestigious societies, including the National Academy of Medicine, and had a consistent record of winning large research grants, as well as substantial contracts for drug development from pharmaceutical companies. Not only was he the best-funded faculty member at MTRI, but he also had the largest research group, with almost thirty postdoctoral researchers. Even with his funding, I couldn't figure out how he could afford that much salary money. It would be interesting to see how he did it; presumably, many of his postdocs had their own fellowships. I was going to start looking at their funding sources when there was another knock on the door and Anna showed Carlson in.

He came through the door with a big smile and an outstretched hand. "Dr. Parker, it's a pleasure to welcome you here. And an honor for me to greet you on the first day of your new job. I think I can speak for all the faculty in wishing you the very best here at MTRI."

I stayed seated behind my desk as he crossed the room and stood in front of me. He was about my height—just under six feet—but with a potbelly that I'd managed to avoid. At least so far.

Ignoring his still-offered hand, I nodded toward an uncomfortable-looking wooden chair I'd placed in front of the desk for the occasion. "Take a seat, Carlson."

His smile faded as he realized that I hadn't asked him here for a social call. I stared at him without speaking until he became visibly uncomfortable. Finally, he broke the silence. "Is there something you wanted to talk with me about?"

"I was at Carolyn Gelman's seminar yesterday. I saw you there, too."

His smile returned. "Ah, yes. Typical shabby performance from her. I'm glad you had a chance to hear for yourself; she's a problem we need you to deal with."

I'd been about to lay into him, but maybe I could learn something first. I changed tactics. "I'm aware that there's a problem. What do you need from me?" I asked.

"Isn't it obvious? We have two candidates coming up for tenure, her and Mark Heller. Mark's fantastic while Gelman's a loser. As our new director, we need you to follow the lead of the faculty and make a clear recommendation for Mark and against Gelman."

"You're aware that there's no reason they couldn't both get tenure, aren't you? It doesn't need to be a competition."

"Of course, I'm aware. Do I look like this is my first tenure case? But Gelman doesn't deserve it, and we don't want her here in a permanent position."

I nodded. "I see. Has the MTRI faculty voted on this yet? I didn't see that in the record."

"Not yet. We've known Lowell was leaving, so we thought it would be best to wait until the new director was on board and could participate in the deliberations." He smiled. "Now that you're here, I've taken the liberty of scheduling a meeting for early next week. I'm sure it's on your calendar."

How presumptuous could the guy get? But I refrained from comment. "Good, I'll look forward to it. But you already think that most of the faculty share your opinion of Gelman?"

"Absolutely. She's a very difficult woman. Not at all popular. The fact is, most of us can't wait to get rid of her."

"Difficult? How so?"

He snorted derisively. "In all the ways you can imagine. Arrogant, only interested in her own research, refuses to work with anyone else's students, won't serve on committees. Need I go on?"

"No, I've got the picture. But how about her science? The fact that she's not a good colleague isn't really a basis for denying tenure. Although it's certainly something that I can talk to her about."

"Her science? You said you were at her seminar. It's derivative third-rate garbage. I don't even trust what she presents as being true."

I'd gotten some useful information, but now he'd opened the door to the point of this meeting. Time to get back to it.

I gave him a cold hard stare. "I heard her seminar. I thought she presented some good work. And I also heard your question. It was disgustingly unprofessional. Rude and totally out of place. I want to be clear that I will not tolerate that sort of abusive conduct, from you or anyone else at MTRI. I expect faculty members to treat each other professionally, as colleagues. If anyone can't behave appropriately, they'd do well to look for another position."

He paled beneath my onslaught, but his recovery was quick. "Who the hell do you think you are! I'm the cornerstone of this institution, the best-funded faculty member here. You can't threaten me like that." He snickered. "You're nothing but a temporary acting director. Just what is it you think you can do to me?"

"I'm aware of your funding. A good-sized NIH grant and a contract with a drug company. It's impressive. But I'm also aware that you occupy nearly twice the amount of lab space as can be justified by the amount of money that you bring in. Do you want to push me into reducing your space allocation to a more appropriate level?"

He flushed a deep red. "My space is fully used. I have more than two dozen postdocs in my group, most of whom have independent fellowship funding. The lab isn't supported just by my own grants."

That was the answer I'd expected. And it gave me the ammunition I needed.

"The fellowships your postdocs have pay their salaries, nothing more. They don't bring in the indirect costs we need to provide the facilities and administrative support that's required to run the institute. That only comes from major grants and contracts. My policy for space allocation at MTRI is going to be the same as it is at most other research institutes. Namely, each investigator will be expected to bring in funding with sufficient indirect costs to support his or her assigned lab space. You fall far short of that expectation."

He jumped out of his chair, shaking with rage. "You can't cut my lab space! That would cripple us."

I looked up at him with a mocking smile. "Thank you for coming to see me. I'm sure we understand each other much better now."

Carlson turned and stormed out of the office, slamming the door loudly behind him.

I couldn't suppress a sense of satisfaction as I watched him leave. Being director of MTRI could have some fun in it after all.

7

Anna stuck her head in moments after Carlson left. "Everything okay?"

I smiled at her. "Just fine, why?"

"Well, he ran out in a huff. Just thought I'd better check."

"He did, didn't he? I must have said something he didn't like."

She giggled. "I guess you did. And you seem to have enjoyed it."

"One of those small pleasures of being director," I said. "You don't seem to like him much, do you?"

She shrugged. "He's one of those older males who don't think women belong in science. So no, I'm not a fan."

"I can see that. Speaking of women scientists, could you get hold of Carolyn Gelman? I'd like to see her next."

"Will do. In the meantime, Jim Putnam has been asking to meet with you."

Yes, my associate director. Time to meet him and get an administrative rundown of the place. "Is he here now?"

"He's in his office, just down the hall. He said I could get him whenever you were free."

I got up from my desk. "That's okay, I'll go to him. Just let me know when Gelman's going to come in. In the meantime, you can stock me up with supplies in here."

She looked around. "Are you sure I can't get something to hang on the walls? It looks so empty. Maybe a clock? And I could borrow a couple of pictures of shorebirds from the patient waiting areas."

I followed her gaze around the room. It did have the forlorn look of a vacated apartment. "You're right, it does look pretty bleak." I gave her a smile. "Birds would be great. Go for it."

* * *

Jim Putnam got up to greet me with a big grin when I knocked and entered through his open office door. "Brad Parker, I assume? Welcome; I'm pleased to meet you."

He was tall and thin, with a full head of red hair. Probably in his mid-forties, a bit young to be in this type of administrative support position.

We shook hands. "And I you. Dan Lowell told me you were invaluable as associate director, on top of all the administrative details. I'm looking forward to getting a rundown."

"Happy to oblige. Where would you like to start?"

"How about with the institute's space plan? Perhaps you can walk me through where the labs of the different faculty are located, and give me a bit of an introduction to what their research profiles are like. Size of their research groups, their funding, that sort of thing."

He nodded. "That's what I figured you'd want to see first. I have it all laid out over here."

We sat at his conference table, which was covered with building plans and spreadsheets. "I made copies of everything for you." He handed me a stack of papers. "The plans show the lab space assigned to each faculty member, and I've put together summaries of their grants and lab personnel. I can flesh things out a bit if you want to talk through it."

I leafed through the documents. Putnam was efficient, for sure. I could see why Lowell had spoken highly of him. "Looks good. Yes, why don't you give me a virtual tour."

"Okay, let's start with the first floor. In addition to you and me, the administrative suite includes offices for our business manager and our grants specialist. I'll introduce you to them later. The rest of the floor is clinical space, including the clinical director's office. More exam rooms and clinical labs on the second floor—again we can visit that later. It's all supported by a big clinical center grant, on which Stan Jacobs—the clinical director—is PI. Then the upper floors are faculty labs and offices. Do you want more info on the clinical operation, or should we move upstairs?"

"Would I be safe to assume the clinic pretty much takes care of itself?"

Putnam nodded. "It does; no problems there."

"Good. I'll get Jacobs to fill me in on the details later. Let's move on to the research."

He spread out plans for the five research floors. Each floor housed the laboratories of four faculty members, together with a shared kitchenette, a conference room, and a common equipment room. Each laboratory was marked with the name of the faculty member to whom the space was assigned, so I could refer to the relevant information on laboratory personnel and funding on the spreadsheet.

With two exceptions, the labs were all about the same size and housed groups of ten or so students and postdoctoral fellows. All of the faculty members at the institute were also well funded, most with sizable NIH grants or the equivalent. There were only two apparent exceptions: Both Tom Carlson and Mark Heller had labs that were nearly twice the size of everyone else's.

"What's going on with Carlson and Heller?" I asked. "They have more space and bigger groups than all the others. It looks like Carlson has a decent grant and some pharmaceutical funding, but not enough to justify all that real estate."

"Carlson has a lot of money that doesn't show up on the spreadsheet. Most of his postdocs are foreign and have fellowships from their home countries. He makes a big thing about running an international lab that's open to anyone good enough to make the grade and bring in their own support. He's got a worldwide reputation, so he attracts a lot of foreign students with their own money."

I wasn't convinced that taking a lot of foreign students just because they had fellowships was a great way to run a lab. It didn't offer much in the way of quality control. But I let that go for now. "And Heller? It looks like most of his funding is from a company called Pharmathor."

"Right, he has a major long-term contract with them. They're the same company that funds Carlson, and I believe Carlson helped him set it up. He's worked with them for years and seems to be connected with some of their execs. Anyway, they funded Heller's development of aloxinor, and now they've given him big bucks to tackle the drug resistance problem."

Interesting. I wondered what would happen to Heller's funding if Carolyn Gelman's approach to drug resistance turned out to be a success. Perhaps he had more reason than tenure to want to put her down.

Before I could pursue that thought, Anna knocked and came in. "Sorry to interrupt, but I just heard back from Carolyn Gelman about meeting."

"Good," I said. "When is she coming in?"

"Sorry; she said her schedule was full today, plus she has to leave early. She suggested Monday afternoon instead. Is that okay, or do you want me to tell her you need to see her today?"

I smiled to myself. So she was too busy to meet with the new director, even though she must know I was about to play an important role in deciding her fate. It certainly fit with what Lowell and Carlson had said about her being self-centered.

"Monday afternoon will be fine," I told Anna. "Just set a time and put it on my calendar."

I had another thought as she turned to leave. "One other thing. Could you send out an email to all the senior faculty on my behalf? Just say that I've decided to postpone the meeting Carlson scheduled to discuss tenure cases next week until I've had a chance to familiarize myself with the candidates."

She smiled. "Sure thing, boss."

Anna didn't say much, but I had a distinct feeling that she knew what was going on. And that she was firmly planted in Gelman's corner. Seemed reasonable enough, but I wasn't ready to take sides yet.

I turned back to Putnam. "Looks like I'm yours for the moment. Why don't we take a look at the institute budget? Then you can introduce me to the other administrative staff and the clinical director."

8

The house on Drakes Island, just north of Wells Beach, was only about ten minutes from MTRI. I got there just before five, when we were scheduled to meet the realtor, and found Karen's red Volvo already parked in the driveway. No Karen, so I walked around the house and found her and Rosie sitting on the back deck looking out at the ocean. My heart gave a familiar flutter as I watched Karen's long blond hair falling around her shoulders in the afternoon breeze.

I went over to greet her with a hug and a kiss, while Rosie jumped up and down clawing at my legs for attention. I bent down to pet her and then looked around. Our deck led right to the beach, where seagulls and sandpipers were busy frolicking in the waves.

"Nice back here, don't you think?" Karen said.

"The location's great, and the beach is beautiful. Now we just need to get in and look at the house."

"No problem, I'm here," a voice behind us said. It belonged to a tall thin man who introduced himself as Martin from Ocean Realty. He proceeded to lead us back around to the front of the house, unlocked the door, and gave us a quick tour. It had an open floor plan with lots of windows featuring panoramic ocean views, and of course a sliding door leading from the living room out to the deck. The furniture looked comfortable, as did the master bedroom upstairs. There was even a fenced-in area of the yard that Rosie could call her own.

"Looks good to me," Karen said.

I added my agreement, and Martin said, "Excellent. I'll leave you to it then. I think you'll find everything you need in the kitchen, and there should be plenty of towels and so forth upstairs. If there's anything you need, just give me a call."

Karen melted into my arms when he left. We kissed deeply, lingering as we pressed against each other.

"I've missed you," I said.

"Me, too. But we have each other for the next couple of days."

"Having each other sounds good. Shall we go check out the bedroom?"

She laughed. "Not yet—I'm hungry. Let's have a drink and something to eat first."

"All right, I've heard that good things come to those who wait. Did you bring Rosie's food? We can feed her and then go to Hobbs."

"I remember Hobbs from last summer," she said. "Good lobster and right nearby in Wells Harbor. But let's save it for another time. This is our first night in our new house on the beach. Let's make dinner here."

"Sounds fine, but I didn't get anything to eat. I guess we can make a quick grocery store run."

She gave me a big grin. "I stopped and picked up a few things in Ogunquit. Come help me bring stuff in from the car."

A trip to the car produced everything we needed. Lobsters, French bread, and salad fixings—not to mention brie for an appetizer, a bottle of wine for Karen, and scotch for me. My favorite Oban, no less.

We fed Rosie and then took bread, cheese, and drinks out to the deck. I sipped scotch and enjoyed the ocean view while Karen spread brie generously on a chunk of bread and dug in. When she finished, she said, "I've got some news about your video recording. My guys couldn't see the face, of course, but they did come up with an estimate of the intruder's build."

"How'd they manage that?"

"Not so hard. There was a table in the background, so they used that to get the scale. They figure the perp is around five foot six, average build, maybe a hundred and forty pounds."

"Nice; that could help. I've only seen Mark Heller sitting down. I don't know if that fits him or not."

"It doesn't," she said. "I checked his driver's license. He's a big guy. Six foot one, weighs over two hundred."

"I guess there's another possibility, isn't there? Could it be a tall woman?"

"Sure. Do you have somebody in mind?"

"Carolyn Gelman. At least some of the faculty seem to think that she sabotaged her own freezer, with the intent of blaming Heller for it."

"You really think she'd try to destroy her own research?"

"I don't know. I haven't had the chance to meet her yet. But I did see her giving a seminar. She's tall."

"Hang on a minute, let me check her license." Karen went into the house and returned with her laptop. She fiddled with it briefly. "You're right. Gelman's five foot five, a hundred thirty-five pounds."

I took a pull of scotch. "So, she's a possible. Kind of hard to swallow, but I can't ignore it. I suppose she could have planned a late-night trip to the lab and rescued the samples before they were ruined."

Karen spread cheese on another piece of bread. "The tape does raise another question, though. Whoever it was took pains to keep their face covered, suggesting they knew the security camera was there. If it was Gelman, would she have tried to blame Heller, when he's such an obvious mismatch to her build?"

"Interesting point. But she may not have realized it would be possible to estimate the intruder's height and weight from the video. I'm meeting with her Monday afternoon, maybe I can get a better feel for her then."

Karen nodded. "Sounds good. In the meantime, hunger's getting to me."

I stood up and turned to go in. "I saw a lobster pot in the kitchen. I'll get some water boiling."

She came up behind me and put her arms around me, pressing her body tight against mine. "No, I meant a different kind of hunger. Let's go check out the bed."

She took my hand and I happily followed her upstairs.

9

He wasn't surprised by the ringtone of the burner phone. He'd been expecting a call from the boss for weeks, ever since the freezer sabotage had been aborted by some random student who came in at the wrong time. At first, the boss told him to lie low, explaining that Gelman's efforts to put the blame on Heller were so self-destructive that it looked like she would do herself in without any further action being necessary.

He hadn't believed it. Direct action was always better, always what it came down to in the end. So he'd waited for new instructions. He smiled as he answered the phone, feeling the first rush of adrenaline at what he imagined would be a call to action.

As usual, the boss spoke through a voice changer. It gave his voice a robotic sound. Or her voice. He had no way of even knowing whether the boss was a man or a woman. Just someone on the phone who gave orders and paid well when they were carried out.

"We need you to get back in the game," the boss said. "Things were going well, but the institute has a new director who seems to give some credence to Gelman. He's even postponed the faculty vote that would have sealed her fate until he studies the case further."

"I understand. Whatever you need."

"It's time for something more definitive. You have the white powder?"

"Of course. Do you want me to use it on Gelman?"

"No, that would be too obvious. I want you to administer it to one of the patients in her clinical trial. Having an unexplained toxic death on her hands should do the trick. Think you can handle that?"

"No problem. Can you get me the patients' names and addresses?" He paused for a moment. "Also the names and addresses of their employers and emergency contacts."

"I'll email it to you shortly. But why the job and emergency contact information?"

"I'm going to have to visit the home to dispense the powder, so I want to pick someone who's employed and lives alone. They'll have emergency contacts living somewhere else and most likely be away at work during the day."

* * *

The email came less than fifteen minutes later. He studied the list, first looking for addresses that appeared to be single-family homes in relatively sparsely populated areas. Then he noted employment, and finally scanned the emergency contacts to narrow the list to patients who probably lived alone. It didn't take long to get it down to a short list of half a dozen. He amused himself by closing his eyes and blindly choosing his victim.

It was six thirty on a Friday evening. The patient he'd chosen was a waitress, so she'd probably be at work serving dinner. May as well get it done.

He put on the brown UPS uniform he'd purchased on eBay for occasions when a disguise might be useful. Then he put on metal-framed glasses and a blond wig. Satisfied that the change in his appearance was adequate, he went over to his dresser and opened the top drawer to retrieve a small vial of white powder that was tucked in the back corner. Thallium sulfate. A deadly poison that had been used in pesticides until the early seventies. As well as in a number of murders.

He drove carefully to the vicinity of his chosen victim's home, which was in a sparsely populated area of Wells. The home of Mrs. Emily Weston, who was sixty-three years old, worked at an Italian restaurant in York, and gave a cousin in New Hampshire as her emergency contact.

When he neared his destination, he pulled off the road and left his car in a parking lot that seemed to be used by hikers. Then he walked half a mile along a wooded road, passing two other houses before he reached his target. The driveway was empty and the house was dark, so he went up to the front door and rang the bell. He was carrying a brown cardboard box—if anyone was home, he'd just be a UPS driver who'd gone to the wrong address.

No one answered the bell, so he knocked loudly. When there was still no answer, he used his lock pick to let himself in. Then he paused and waited. This was the tricky moment, there'd be no good way of explaining himself if someone suddenly appeared. But that didn't happen. He was alone.

The house was a small ranch. Two bedrooms, one of which appeared to be a guest room. The one that was in use had an attached bath, and a bottle of pills with an MTRI label was sitting on the counter. What could be easier? Even better, there were only three pills in the bottle.

He removed one of the capsules from the bottle and emptied its contents into the toilet. Then he refilled the capsule from the vial of white powder in his pocket and replaced it in the bottle. The label said to take one of the pills each morning.

Mrs. Weston would have the bad luck of starting one of the next three days by taking the wrong capsule.

10

Karen took off before eight on Monday morning, in time for her to make a ten o'clock meeting back at FBI headquarters in Chelsea. My plan was to spend today and tomorrow making the rounds of the MTRI faculty members, including Gelman and Heller but the others as well. Just a series of informal visits so that I could introduce myself and chat with each of them about their work and whatever administrative concerns they might have. Most of those conversations would undoubtedly include the two pending tenure cases, but you never knew what else might be going on. Unless you asked.

Anna greeted me with an open box of Congdon's donuts when I got to the institute. "Happy Monday," she said, as I thanked her and carefully selected an apple fritter. I remembered Congdon's from when Karen and I were here last summer. They were a Wells institution, and I had no argument with their claim to serving America's best donuts.

Another pleasant surprise greeted me when I opened the door to my office. There was a rubber plant in the corner next to the conference table, a clock hanging opposite my desk, and two paintings of shorebirds on the walls. I recognized one as the sandpipers I was familiar with from Wells Beach and was examining the other when Anna came in behind me.

"Piping plovers," she said. "Could you tell?"

I gave her a grateful smile. "I recognized the sandpipers, but I wasn't sure about these guys. They're endangered, but they nest on the beaches here, right? Thanks for doing all this, it looks great."

She beamed at the praise. "My pleasure. It needed something. Is where I put the clock okay?"

"Yep. Just right for me to look at when a meeting's running too long and I need to give someone the signal that time's up."

She grinned. "That's what I figured. Speaking of meetings, Dr. Gelman is scheduled to come in at two this afternoon. Is there anything else I can do for you?"

"Thanks, I'm good for now. I'm going to spend a few hours going around the institute and introducing myself to some of the faculty. Just dropping by their offices for informal chats with whoever has time."

* * *

It was one thirty before I got back to my office. Just enough time to review Carolyn Gelman's file once more before our two o'clock meeting. My tour had connected me with seven different faculty members. Back-to-back meetings with that many people was exhausting, but it had been worthwhile. Not only could I start putting names together with faces and personalities, but I'd gotten a preliminary sense of how people felt about the Heller and Gelman cases.

As I'd expected, nobody had any question about Heller. The universal opinion was that he was a superstar and a sure bet for tenure. On the other hand, my new colleagues' views on Gelman were decidedly mixed.

Three of them, two men and one woman, were strongly opposed, with opinions similar to what I'd heard from Carlson. In their views, Gelman was a poor colleague who refused to participate in institute activities. They thought her work was potentially interesting, but still very preliminary. It was clear that at least two of them were strongly influenced by Carlson in reaching that conclusion. Ann Osborne—the woman who'd aggressively questioned Gelman at her seminar—made Carlson's influence abundantly clear when she asked if I'd been at the seminar. When I responded affirmatively, she said, "Then you heard what Carlson thinks. If he doesn't trust her work, neither do I."

Two others were solidly in Gelman's corner. While acknowledging that Heller's case was stronger, they felt that Gelman did good work and was above the bar for promotion for tenure. They wanted to support her, as long as doing so wouldn't jeopardize Heller's chances—which I assured them it wouldn't. When I asked what they thought about Carlson's criticism of her work, one just rolled his eyes and said, "Not much." The other was a bit more expansive. "Carlson's coming at this from two sides, both highly prejudicial," she said. "On the one hand, Heller's his golden boy. On the other, he's a misogynist who thinks women belong at home. Not in science. Thank God there aren't many like him left. At least not as many as there used to be."

The remaining two were on the fence. They acknowledged but were willing to overlook the fact that Gelman wasn't a great colleague. However, they didn't know what to think about her work. It seemed fine as far as they could tell. But if someone like Carlson didn't trust her, how could they have the confidence needed to support promotion to tenure? They wanted to hear what people had to say at a full faculty meeting before reaching a decision.

With this kind of split in the faculty, the meeting to discuss and vote on the two tenure cases would be critical. I was glad that

I'd postponed it. Carlson would obviously play a strong role, and I needed to be prepared to provide whatever counterbalance was necessary to keep the proceedings fair.

But first, I needed to figure out where I stood. And the next step—talking to Gelman—was about to happen.

Anna knocked on my door a few minutes before two. Good; Gelman was right on time. I stood up to greet her and told Anna to show her in.

"I'm sorry," Anna said. "She just called. She's not coming."

I stopped dead in my tracks. Was she crazy? What in hell was she thinking to blow off a scheduled meeting with her new director?

"She sounded pretty frantic," Anna continued. "One of the patients in her trial got terribly sick and has been rushed to the emergency room. Dr. Gelman's gone to the hospital to be with her."

I calmed down. She would naturally be concerned about an emergency involving one of her patients. But cancelling a meeting with me, especially one that could be key to her future, didn't fit the picture of Gelman as a cold self-centered woman that her colleagues had painted. I wondered if she was genuinely worried about her patient, or if her concern was a more selfish focus on how an unexpected complication would impact her trial…and her obviously faltering bid for tenure.

There was one way to find out. Which might give me more insight into Carolyn Gelman than I'd get from a formal meeting.

"What hospital are they at?" I asked.

"York Hospital, why?"

I'd seen signs for it on US 1, a few miles south of Ogunquit. Maybe a fifteen- or twenty-minute drive.

"I'm going to go find Gelman there. See if she needs anything."

I started to leave, then had an afterthought. "What's the patient's name? I'll need it to locate them in the ER."

"Emily Weston," Anna said.

11

I headed south on US 1 through Ogunquit to York, where I turned off just before the entrance to I-95 and made my way to York Hospital. It was located on a street called Loving Kindness Way, which pretty much epitomized the hospital's atmosphere. Rather than the towering structures of hospitals in Boston, York Hospital was a two-story brick building with the welcoming look of a country inn. Inside the main entrance, I was greeted by a smiling woman at a concierge desk. When I said that I was looking for a patient recently admitted to the emergency room, she asked for the patient's name and then directed me across the hall to a softly lit waiting room that featured a large fish tank and Maine coastal seascapes on the walls.

In contrast to the frenetic crowding in the emergency rooms I'd visited before, there were only two people there, sitting on opposite sides of the room in comfortable-looking overstuffed chairs. I recognized one of them as Carolyn Gelman. She was sitting rigidly straight, staring blankly at the entrance to the ER across from her. Worry was written all over her face.

I went over and introduced myself. It seemed to take a moment for her to recognize my name. Then her eyes widened and she said, "Dr. Parker? What…what are you doing here?"

I sat down next to her. "My admin told me that one of your patients became unexpectedly ill, and that you were here with her.

I thought I'd come down and see if there was anything I could do to help."

Her eyes moistened and she gave me a tentative smile. "That's so kind of you. I certainly didn't expect you to do that. Thank you."

Since none of her other colleagues were here, I could see why she was surprised to see me. "I'll be happy to do whatever I can. Tell me what's going on."

"It's Emily, Emily Weston. She was one of the first patients to start in my trial, around six months ago. And she's been doing so well. Her cancer went into remission, and it's stayed there. No sign of emerging drug resistance." Her lower lip started to tremble and tears formed. "And now this."

Gelman didn't seem like the hard-hearted bitch her colleagues had described to me. I reached over and tentatively squeezed her arm. "I'm so sorry. What's happened?"

"I apologize for breaking down like this." She paused and took a deep breath. "She said it started with nausea and vomiting around eleven this morning. Then she started having severe stomach pains. She said they got worse and worse until she couldn't stand it anymore, at which point she called 911. They sent an ambulance and brought her here, which is when they called me. She's also having trouble breathing now, and they're not sure what's going on. Food poisoning maybe. They're going to admit her and get her into a room shortly."

"I hate to ask this, but do you think it could be drug toxicity?"

"I don't know. Obviously, I'm terrified of that." Her hands started trembling again. "She's such a nice woman, I feel terrible. But it seems odd—she hasn't had any side effects until this. Why so suddenly? And so severe?"

I tried to be reassuring. "Don't blame yourself. If she hasn't had previous problems, it's probably not the drugs. Food poisoning sounds more likely."

She tried to smile, but it didn't quite come off. "You're very kind."

She didn't say it, but I was pretty sure that being treated kindly wasn't something she was used to.

"Can I get you anything?" I asked. "Coffee or something to eat?"

"Thank you, but I don't want anything. I'll just stay here, at least until her cousin comes. That's her emergency contact, he lives in Concord, New Hampshire."

"I can stay with you, if you'd like."

There were tears in her eyes again when she looked at me. "That's really very nice of you. But you don't have to; I'll be all right. My husband's managed to leave work early to pick up the kids and feed them tonight."

"All right." I wrote my cell phone number on a piece of paper and handed it to her. "Keep me posted, and don't hesitate to call if there's anything I can do."

She managed another weak smile as I left, hoping that I'd been able to offer some comfort. I'd learned a lot from the visit. My take was that Carolyn Gelman was sensitive and empathetic, far from being the self-centered bitch her detractors portrayed. And from her evident surprise at my attention, she was also a woman who seemed unused to anyone offering support. I wondered if that applied to her husband, as well as to her colleagues. There was something about the way she said that he'd take care of the kids tonight that made it sound like that didn't happen often. If that were true and she bore the brunt of responsibility at home, she'd have no choice but to keep a rigid schedule and a clear sense of priorities at work.

The woman at the reception desk smiled as I passed her on my way out. "How's Mrs. Weston doing?"

"I'm afraid we're not really sure," I said. "I believe they're moving her to a room now."

"So sad. She must be a nice woman, to have so many people worried about her. You, that sweet Dr. Gelman, and now her brother just called. He sounds like a nice man."

That seemed odd. Carolyn had said that the emergency contact was a cousin.

"Don't you mean her cousin?" I asked.

"No, her cousin called earlier. This was her brother, said he lives nearby in Sanford. It was odd, though, he didn't sound like a Mainer. He had a funny accent."

"Like what?"

"I don't really know. Maybe Russian. I'm from New York; I used to go to a Russian restaurant there."

A brother with a Russian accent who wasn't the emergency contact? Weird. I'd have to remember to ask Carolyn about him.

12

Tuesday was the first morning I woke up alone in the Drakes Island house. Well, alone except for Rosie. It took a minute for me to get oriented before I shuffled into the kitchen to make coffee and let Rosie out into her yard. Then I took my coffee out to the deck and started checking email.

A message from Carolyn was already waiting.

Thanks again for your support yesterday. I really appreciate it. My patient is stable this morning, but now complaining of pain in her feet. Still having trouble breathing. I'm going to go back to the hospital soon. Can we reschedule the meeting we were supposed to have yesterday?

I thanked her for the update and told her that I was going to be in Boston for the rest of the week after today, but Anna would be in touch to reschedule. In the meantime, I added, don't hesitate to let me know if you need anything.

That left the day open for more visits with MTRI faculty, including Mark Heller, whom Anna had scheduled to meet with me in my office this afternoon. I wanted formal meetings with him and Carolyn as tenure candidates, rather than the casual drop-ins I was doing with the other faculty members. Except for Tom Carlson, with whom I'd already spent more time than I wanted to.

Unfortunately, that's who was sitting in my outer office when I got to MTRI. Anna looked apologetic, but Carlson was on his feet as soon as I opened the door. "Sorry to intrude, but I need a word with you. It's somewhat urgent."

The lack of any kind of pleasantry was notable but not surprising, given our last meeting. I remained equally aloof as I let him into my office and sat behind my desk, indicating that he should take a chair across from me. "What's on your mind?"

"I've heard that one of the patients in Gelman's trial is acutely ill. It sounds like severe toxicity. I'm bringing it to your attention so that you can terminate the trial immediately."

"I'm aware of the situation, and I've spoken with Gelman. It's not clear what's wrong with the patient; it may simply be food poisoning. Gelman says that the patient has been in the trial for six months and has been doing well, with no side effects. I don't see any reason to assume this is drug toxicity."

Carlson's eyes flared. "I heard that the patient presented with severe nausea and vomiting. You don't see any reason to think that's drug toxicity? What more classic side effects of cancer treatment could you be looking for?"

"I understand, although those problems are much less common in patients like Gelman's who are receiving targeted therapies rather than standard chemotherapeutic drugs. And again, this particular patient has been taking the same drugs without a problem for months."

He turned red and rose out of his chair to lean over the desk. "Bullshit! I don't understand why you're defending her. Your duty is to the institute, which means protecting our patients and reputation. You need to shut Gelman down before she kills somebody."

I struggled to control my temper as I got up to face him. "Why do I feel like you have an ulterior motive here? What do you have against Gelman that warrants this kind of behavior?"

"I just want you to do your damn job!"

"I intend to. By seeing that all of our faculty are treated fairly and objectively." I sat back down and turned my attention to some papers on my desk. That failed to make him disappear, so I looked up after a while and said, "You can leave now."

He stomped out, slamming the door even louder than he had after his last visit. It was getting to be a habit.

* * *

I'd completed my rounds of most of the remaining faculty members by the time I was scheduled to meet with Mark Heller. Their views of Carolyn Gelman were pretty evenly divided, mirroring what I'd heard the day before. Somewhat surprisingly, the news about her stricken patient had traveled fast. Several of the people I talked to asked me about it, and two of them echoed Carlson in suggesting that I shut down the trial—albeit less venomously. They seemed satisfied with my explanation for why I didn't think the patient's illness was drug toxicity and let the matter drop. Still, I was left with a lingering sense that they didn't really believe me and were just waiting for the next piece of bad news.

Why was Gelman so widely disliked? The woman I'd met yesterday seemed pleasant enough. Sure, I could see where pressures from work and home would collide to make her focus on her professional priorities and avoid the kind of institutional chores that other faculty members seemed to resent her sloughing off. But did that really explain why roughly half of her colleagues wanted to destroy her career? Or was Carlson influential enough to have so decisively swayed faculty opinion against her, for whatever reasons he had?

I had to admit that I was viscerally on Gelman's side after meeting her yesterday. I certainly couldn't imagine that the woman I'd seen in the ER waiting room had sabotaged her own freezer. But how much I could or should try to influence the upcoming tenure decision was a different question. One that I was still pondering when Anna knocked on the door and showed Mark Heller into my office.

Time to meet everyone's golden boy.

13

Heller wore a blue blazer, a white button-down shirt, and a confident smile for the occasion. I got up to meet him, and he greeted me with a firm handshake, the smile broadening as he looked down at me from his six-foot-one height advantage. I was surprised by the difference a couple of inches made.

He started to take a chair opposite my desk, but I motioned him across to the conference table. “Let’s sit over here. It’s less formal than looking at each other across a desk.”

He put a laptop that he’d brought with him on the table as he sat down. “Great. I appreciate your taking the time to meet with me.”

I began with my standard lead-in to interviews with tenure candidates. “I make a point of meeting personally with junior faculty who are coming up for tenure. I’ve found it’s important for me to get a better sense of tenure candidates than just what’s on paper. I realize this kind of chat can be pretty formal and off-putting for you, but the point is simply for me to have an opportunity to talk with you about your work and your goals for the future. And also about your experience here at MTRI. It’s my chance to get to know you as a person rather than just a CV. And, of course, I’m also happy to answer any questions you might have about the tenure evaluation process.” I smiled. “I can still remember back when I was up for tenure. The whole thing seemed scary and mysterious, basically my whole life was on the line, and I didn't really know what was going on. That seems like unnecessary pain and suffering—so I'd be happy to offer any clarification on the evaluation process or address any concerns that you have."

"Thanks. I appreciate your openness, but I'm fine with the process." He shrugged. "Maybe a little nervous, but my work speaks for itself, and the senior faculty here have been very supportive. So I don't have any issues, and I'm sure the tenure thing will go smoothly. But I'm happy to have the chance to tell you about my work. You missed my tenure seminar, didn't you?"

"I'm impressed by your confidence." I didn't say what I was really thinking—that he seemed so over-confident as to be best described as cocky. "And yes, I did miss your tenure seminar. I believe it was the week before I started here. So tell me, how did you get into your line of research?"

Instead of answering, he opened the laptop. "Why don't I just take you through my seminar? I'm sure it'll answer all your questions." He pulled up a PowerPoint presentation and turned the computer to face me. The title slide read "Curing Cancer Today." Nothing modest about that.

I really wanted an informal discussion, not a formal lecture. But I didn't want to be overbearing, so I tried to turn him around gently. "Thanks, but I've been through your file and read your recent papers. I probably don't need your whole seminar, but I would like to get more of an intuitive feel for how you approach research questions."

He smiled and plowed right ahead with the PowerPoint, as if he hadn't heard. "Oh, it's no problem. It'll be easy enough to just take you through this."

With that he moved to the second slide and I sat back and listened. It was either that or cut him off more forcefully, which I decided would be unpleasantly rude. I interrupted with a couple of questions, but mostly he spent the next fifty-odd minutes working methodically through a full-blown seminar for his captive audience of one. As I already knew, it was an impressive story of successful drug development. But it was delivered with much more formality and at far greater length than I needed to hear.

I struggled to avoid squirming in my chair and suppressed a sigh of relief when he finally finished. "Very impressive. So tell me, your major thrust now is dealing with the drug resistance problem?"

"That's right. The company behind aloxinor, Pharmathor, has given us a substantial contract to develop derivatives that would still target cancers that become resistant to the original drug. We already have two such compounds that I hope will be ready to enter clinical trials soon."

"Very nice. I assume your derivatives work on cancers that become resistant as a result of mutations in the RTK that aloxinor targets?"

"Yes, that's correct."

"How about cancers that become resistant by other mechanisms, like changes in parallel or downstream pathways? Can you estimate what fraction of resistance is due to mutations in the original aloxinor target?"

The cocky smile faded. He knew where I was going with this. "About fifty percent of resistance is due to mutations in the original target. Dealing with those would be a very major advance."

"It certainly would. But what do you think of Carolyn Gelman's approach, which would also work on cancers that become resistant by other mechanisms?"

I could tell the question struck home as he flushed momentarily. But his recovery was quick. "I suppose it's an interesting idea, but the data she has are pretty shaky. I believe you were at her seminar?"

I nodded and he continued. "Then you saw that people don't really believe her work. And I've heard that one of the patients in her trial has developed a severe toxic reaction, which sounds like a big problem."

It was an ugly way for him to portray the work of a colleague, but I wasn't going to get into that with him. "It's true that one of her patients is ill, but I'm not at all sure that it's a case of drug toxicity." I glanced up at the clock that Anna had strategically placed on the wall. "Anyway, it's getting late and I also wanted to ask how you feel you've been treated during your time at MTRI. Have the senior faculty been supportive as you've worked to develop your career? Have there been any problems you'd like to bring to my attention?"

"My senior colleagues have been great. The only problem I've had has been with Gelman."

"Because she's working on aloxinor resistance?"

"Partly that, yes. She's tried to push in on my success. But worse, she keeps attacking me, hinting to people that I'm trying to interfere with her work. She's even said that she suspects me of sabotaging her lab and unplugging her freezer."

I sat back and pursed my lips. "I've heard that, although not from her. What do you think happened?"

He shrugged. "Who knows? But I can assure you, I had nothing to do with it."

At least on that point, I knew from Karen's analysis of the video that he was telling the truth. But I decided to see what would happen if I pushed a little. "I certainly hope not. Where were you when it happened?"

He sat up rigidly straight. "They say it was after midnight, when I was home asleep. Why are you asking me that? The cops already interviewed me."

"Just curious. I was wondering if you had an alibi that would put any rumors of your involvement to rest. Was anyone with you?"

"I'm afraid not. I live alone."

"Too bad." I shrugged. "Hopefully the cops will figure it out soon."

"Do you really think I'd do something like that?"

I didn't tell him that I was the only one who knew that he hadn't. Besides Karen. And of course, whoever the saboteur actually was. But I did offer some reassurance. "Don't worry; I can't imagine you'd do anything that stupid. And I'd certainly never suspect you without evidence."

He exhaled deeply. "Thanks. I was starting to get nervous. I hope I can count on your support."

"I can't make any guarantees, but I don't think you have anything to worry about," I said. "Your record speaks for itself."

The confident smile returned as he said goodbye and left.

14

By five in the afternoon, I'd picked up Rosie and we were headed back to Boston on I-95. Unless the traffic was a mess, we'd be home by six thirty or so. I texted Karen, who said that she and dinner would be ready and waiting. And not to worry if Boston traffic did its usual job on estimated travel times.

My phone rang as I was approaching Kittery, the last exit in Maine before crossing the Piscataqua River into New Hampshire. I couldn't think of anybody besides Karen who might be calling, so I pulled over to the side of the road and checked the phone. The call was from the Maine area code with a number I didn't recognize. Maybe Anna calling about something at MTRI?

Since I'd already pulled over, I took the call. The voice on the other end was unsteady and the words came out in a rush.

"Dr. Parker, it's Carolyn. Carolyn Gelman. I'm so sorry to bother you. I…I've just had some terrible news."

Had that asshole Carlson pulled something on her?

"Carolyn, calm down. It's fine that you called. What's going on?"

"It's my patient, Emily Weston. You remember, in York Hospital."

So not Carlson. But maybe worse.

"Of course I remember. Is something wrong?"

"Yes, it's horrible." She was having trouble getting the words out between sobs. "She's gotten worse. She's having trouble breathing and they've moved her to intensive care."

"My God! I'm so sorry. Are you at the hospital? I'm close by; I can meet you there if you want."

"No, I'm at home. The kids are here and my husband's stuck in Portland, so I can't leave. There's nothing I could do at the hospital anyway."

"Is there anything I can do to help?"

There was a pause on the other end of the line. "I hate to ask this, but could you come over? I…I just need someone to talk to. This is so awful…what if she dies? I feel terrible."

She sounded desperate. And she must be if she had to ask me, really no more than a stranger, for support. Were there no friends she could talk to? And was her husband so busy that he couldn't be there when she needed him in an emergency?

So much for my trip to Boston.

"Of course I'll come over, no problem at all. I'm in Kittery now, but I'll be there as soon as I can."

Her sigh of relief was audible. "Oh, thank you. Thank you so much. We're in Kennebunkport, I'll text you the address."

I called Karen while I waited for Carolyn's text. She was less than thrilled, and even more so when I told her that this might mess up the rest of the week, not just tonight. Depending on what was happening with Carolyn's patient, I might need to stay at MTRI and deal with the fallout rather than going back to Boston. But, as usual, she understood.

"Do what you need to do," she said. "I'll come back up Friday afternoon anyway. You owe me a big lobster dinner at Hobbs after this."

Carolyn texted me an address on Ocean Avenue in Kennebunkport. Google Maps told me it was about forty-five minutes away, apparently right on the ocean. I got off the highway at the Kittery exit and turned around, heading back north on I-95 to Wells. Then I got off and took US 1 and Route 9 to Kennebunkport, where I found Ocean Avenue and proceeded to Carolyn's address. Which turned out to be less than a mile from the Bush family compound on Walker's Point.

The house was a large contemporary with lots of glass, sitting on a rocky cliff overlooking the ocean. Maybe not as spectacular as the Bush compound, but not too shabby. I remembered that Carolyn's husband was a lawyer. He must do well—no way Carolyn could afford this on an academic's salary.

Carolyn opened the door before I had a chance to ring the bell. Her eyes were red and her hand was trembling as she took mine in greeting. "Thank you so much for coming. I just didn't know who else I could call."

"It's not a problem, I'm happy I could stop by. Are your kids here? A boy and a girl, right?"

"I finally got hold of the sitter, and she was able to take them for the night." She shook her head sadly. "First good thing that's happened all day. How'd you know I have a boy and a girl?"

"It's in your file somewhere. How's the patient doing?"

"I haven't heard anything more. They promised to call if there's any news. Can you come sit with me?"

I followed her into the living room and she motioned me to a cream-colored leather couch in front of a sliding door leading to the deck and the ocean. She started to sit across from me, but interrupted herself. "Can I get you a drink or something?"

I didn't want to make this a social call, but she looked like she could use something. Although she also looked like she might already have had one too many. I left the door open. "I'll join you, if you'd like one. Whatever you're having will be fine."

Her phone rang before she made it to the kitchen. She grabbed it, and I watched her face fall as she listened. The tears were flowing when she hung up. "She's worse, they had to put her on a ventilator. They...they said I needed to come now if I want to see her."

I got up and put my hands on her shoulders. "Let's go. I'll drive."

She took my left hand and squeezed it. "Thank you. Thank you for being here."

Rosie started jumping up and down in the front seat as soon as she saw us leave the house. I'd almost forgotten she was waiting in the car. "Sorry, I have my dog with me," I said to Carolyn. "Hope that's okay."

She tried a smile. Without much success. "It's fine. I like dogs."

We got in, and after greeting me, Rosie turned to Carolyn. With that sixth sense dogs have, she knew how upset Carolyn was. When Carolyn ventured to pet her, Rosie hopped into her lap, licked her hand, and snuggled up to her. And so the three of us made our way to York Hospital. I drove as fast as I could, Carolyn stared out the window and absently rubbed Rosie's head, and Rosie offered whatever comfort licks and snuggles could provide.

Inside the main entrance, we were greeted by the same woman at the concierge desk who'd been there yesterday. When we told her that we were here for Emily Weston, her face filled with concern. She asked us to wait while she called Dr. Ashland.

Perhaps ten minutes passed, with Carolyn growing increasingly nervous, before a middle-aged woman in blue scrubs approached us. "I'm Dr. Ashland. You're here for Mrs. Weston?"

Carolyn nodded. "I'm Dr. Gelman. She's my patient, in my clinical trial. Can we see her?"

Instead of answering, Ashland looked at me with a raised eyebrow.

"I'm Dr. Parker, director of MTRI," I explained. "I assume you know that your patient is enrolled in one of our lung cancer trials, which Dr. Gelman is leading."

"I'm aware," Ashland said. "All right, I can take you in briefly. She's unconscious and on a ventilator. I'm afraid things aren't going well."

We followed Ashland to the ICU. There were two beds occupied, one of which had a patient on a ventilator with a nurse hovering around her.

Carolyn went over and stood beside Emily Weston. "I'm so sorry," she said, stroking the patient's forehead. A clump of loose hair fell out.

"Is she losing her hair?" I asked.

The nurse answered. "Yes, the poor thing. We see that all the time with patients on chemo."

We stayed there for several minutes, with Carolyn holding Emily's hand and crying softly. Then Dr. Ashland said that we should go and promised to call if anything changed.

I put my arm around Carolyn for support and the nurse took us back to the main desk. As we approached the entryway, I noticed a short man with long blond hair talking to the woman at the concierge desk. He must have heard us coming, because he glanced over at us before he turned away from the desk and left the hospital.

When we reached the desk, the woman behind it gave us a sympathetic smile. "I'll pray for Mrs. Weston. And you can be sure that she's in the best of hands. It's too bad you missed her brother, he left just a minute ago."

"Is that the man you were talking to?" I asked.

She nodded and I left Carolyn at the desk to see if I could catch him. But by the time I got through the door, he was getting into his car. A black SUV, I thought a Subaru. He drove past me and I waved to get his attention, but he kept going and I watched him pull out of the parking lot.

15

He pulled over to the side of the road just outside the exit from the hospital parking lot and dialed the emergency number. When it went to voice mail, he said, "Sorry, lost dog." The return call came immediately.

"What is it? It better be important for you to use this number," the boss said.

"I'm at York Hospital. The woman they admitted here is going down; they just put her on a ventilator."

"Good. But why are you there? What if someone remembers you?"

"They wouldn't give out information on the phone, I had to come by and pump them. It's all right, nobody could recognize me with the disguise I have on."

"If you say so. It's your neck. Anything else?"

"Yes, that woman Gelman was here. Along with the new MTRI director."

"They were together?"

"Very much so. I saw them in the lobby. He had his arm around her."

The boss was uncharacteristically silent for a moment. Then the muffled voice said, "Are you suggesting that something's going on between them? That would account for the support he's giving her at the institute."

"It certainly seems that way. Shall I look into it?"

"Yes. Let me know."

He kept his eyes on the rearview mirror after the boss ended the call. Good timing: It was only a few minutes before a blue Honda CRV passed by with the Gelman woman in the passenger seat.

He let it get ahead and followed at a safe distance, staying far enough back to avoid being seen. They headed north on US 1, so he guessed they were going to MTRI. But they passed the turnoff on Chapel Road and continued on Route 1. Maybe heading for Parker's house on Drakes Island? But they passed Drakes Island Road, still traveling north on 1.

His pulse quickened. Where were they going? Maybe her house? Still being careful to stay well back, he used his phone to run a quick check of her address. Possible—she lived in Kennebunkport. A fancy address on Ocean Avenue.

When they turned onto Route 9, he guessed he was right and let them get ahead. Traffic was too light to keep them in sight without being spotted. Instead he drove slowly to her house.

Yes, the blue CRV was parked in the driveway.

Maybe something really was *going on.*

He found a place to park down the street where he could just keep the house in sight. Then he got his camera out of the back and settled in to wait.

16

Carolyn sat quietly, alone with her thoughts and with Rosie on her lap, while I drove back to Kennebunkport. I wasn't very good at small talk under the best of circumstances, and the couple of attempts I made fell on deaf ears. Still, from the way she petted Rosie and shot occasional glances in my direction, I could tell she was glad to have us with her.

It was a few minutes after eight when I pulled into her circular driveway and stopped in front of the house. I reached over and squeezed her hand. "If anything happens, give me a call. I'm just going to go home and take care of Rosie—she needs her dinner. Don't hesitate if you need anything."

Her face fell. "Oh, can't you come in? Rosie too, of course. Please, I just can't be alone now."

"Isn't your husband home yet? It's late. I'm sure he'll be here soon if he's not home already."

She looked down at her hands. "He's staying in Portland tonight. I told him what happened, but he can't make it home."

"I'm sorry. I know what important dinner meetings can be like. But I'm sure he'll be home as soon as he's free."

If it was possible, her eyes grew even sadder. "No, the thing is, he has an early-morning meeting tomorrow. He likes to stay there overnight when that happens. He hates having to get up early to travel."

That told me pretty much all I needed to know about her husband. With any luck, I'd never have to meet the selfish bastard. It would be hard to play nice if I did.

"Please, just come in and have a drink." Her voice was pleading. "I'm sure I have something that'll work for Rosie's dinner. I can fix something for us, too, if you'd like."

I smiled reassuringly. "Sure, I'll be happy to. And Rosie thanks you."

We followed her into the house, after Rosie paused briefly to relieve herself on the front lawn. Carolyn went immediately into the kitchen. "Rosie first," she said.

Taking care of her new friend seemed to give Carolyn a sense of purpose. She filled a mixing bowl with water and offered it to Rosie, who gave Carolyn a thank-you kiss before taking an appreciative slurp. Then Carolyn opened the fridge and surveyed its contents. "There's some cold roast chicken. Would she like that?"

"Sounds perfect."

She pulled the chicken out and got a saucer from the dish cabinet. Handing me a knife, she said, "Why don't you fix it for her? You know what she likes."

It didn't take Rosie long to figure out what was happening. By the time I got some chicken cut up, she was bouncing up and down in anticipation. When I put the plate down, she dug in with full pug gusto, snorting and slurping away.

Carolyn actually laughed. "I'm not sure I've ever had such an appreciative dinner guest. How about you? A drink? We've got pretty much everything."

"Scotch would be great if you have some."

She got out a bottle of single malt and poured two healthy glasses. "I don't usually drink the hard stuff, but I think I could use it tonight. Do you want some chicken?"

Without waiting for an answer, she sliced some onto a platter and added half a loaf of French bread. I followed her out to a table on the deck, overlooking a rocky cliff leading down to the ocean.

She sat with her phone in front of her and took a large gulp of scotch. "I keep waiting for the doctor to call. I'm so scared she's going to die."

"All we can do is hope for the best." I took a sip of scotch. "In the meantime, try to relax a bit."

I put some chicken on a chunk of bread and took a bite. More to have something to do than because I felt like eating. "This tastes good," I said. "Have some."

Instead, she took another gulp of scotch. "Thanks, but I think more of this is what I need right now."

Her eyes were turning glassy. I said, "Take it easy. That can hit you fast if you're not used to it."

She gave a half smile and drained her glass. "Wouldn't be so bad if it knocked me out tonight. I'm going to take a pill and try to sleep. Don't worry, just half a pill."

I got up. "All right, no more than that, though. Have a good night. And again, if you need me, just call."

Her face fell. "Oh no, can't you stay?" Then she flushed. "I mean, in the guest room. It's all made up. Please, I'd feel so much better knowing you're here." She looked at her phone. "Just in case anything happens."

The invitation seemed innocent enough, but I wasn't comfortable with a sleepover. Even putting aside the suggestion of sexual impropriety, I was director of her institute and we had to maintain a professional relationship. On the other hand, desperation was written all over her face. She'd already been abandoned by her husband. I couldn't add to the sense of isolation she was obviously feeling.

Against my better judgment, I agreed. I had toiletries and clean clothes that I was taking to Boston in the car, so I excused myself to take Rosie out and get my things. When I came back, she showed me to a nicely furnished room on the second floor.

"I'll be right next door; just holler if you need anything," she said.

I waited long enough to be sure that the sounds from next door were peaceful. Then I got ready for bed and fell asleep with Rosie in her usual position, snuggled next to me. It was a bit strange, but it had been a long day and falling asleep is one of the things I'm good at. Rosie, too, so we slept soundly.

Until I was jolted awake by the feeling of a weight sinking onto the bed next to me. It took a moment for me to realize where I was. And to recognize a weeping Carolyn crawling into bed beside me.

She barely managed to speak between sobs. "She's gone. They just called—she died an hour ago."

I sat up in shock. "Oh no. I'm so sorry."

I reached out to squeeze her shoulder, but she melted into my arms instead. "Just hold me," she whimpered.

She pulled me back down onto the bed and lay with her head on my chest, sobbing in my arms as I held her. I don't know how long we stayed like that, but I must have eventually fallen back to sleep. She was gone when the sun woke me in the morning.

I jumped out of bed and ran downstairs, frightened for her. But she was in the kitchen having coffee. To my surprise, she looked more composed than I'd seen her since yesterday, with her hair brushed and wearing a blue seersucker robe over her pajamas.

When she saw me, she got up and gave me a hug. "Good morning, and thank you. I couldn't have made it through last night without you. I'm sorry that I was such a pain."

I returned the hug, taking care to keep it casual. "Not at all. I'm glad I could be here when you needed someone. You're looking much better, though. Will you be all right now?"

She managed a faint smile. "I've got to hold myself together again. The kids will be home soon. Time to be a mom."

"You'll do it. In the meantime, I'll get out of your hair. No need to explain me to your kids."

She nodded. "There's half an hour before they'll be home. Have some coffee."

I took the coffee upstairs while I cleaned up a bit and got my things. Ten minutes later, I was back downstairs with Rosie.

Carolyn walked us to the door. "Are you going to Boston now?"

"No, I need to go back to MTRI." I didn't want to say why, but I couldn't avoid it much longer. "We'll have to deal with Mrs. Weston's death in the context of your clinical trial."

"I know. We should probably stop the trial until we can figure out what happened to her."

"Maybe… We need to think about it. Will you be going in to work? We can talk about it later."

"Yes, I'll be in after the kids are settled." She opened the door and we stepped out onto the front deck. "Thank you again for last night. So much." She threw her arms around me and held me close for a moment. Then she said, "I'll see you later," and disappeared back inside.

17

He knew he'd been right when Parker came out of the house and got an overnight bag from his car. They were lovers.

It would probably be a long night, but he'd done overnight stake-outs before. Many times, starting back when he was still an agent in the FSB, Russia's successor to the KGB. He took two of his "stay-awake pills" and settled in for the night.

The shots he got of them saying goodbye the next morning were worth the wait. The woman holding him tight, pressing her body against his, wearing nothing but pajamas and a lightweight robe. As if they were teenagers who'd had sex for the first time.

He uploaded the photos to the shared folder on Dropbox and waited. It didn't take long for the phone to buzz.

"So you were right," the boss said. "He spent the night with her?"

"Yes. You like my photography?"

"Indeed, it may prove useful. The woman in the hospital died last night, as well."

"Good. Do you have anything more for me?"

"Not yet. Let's see if this takes care of it."

He checked his watch when the boss ended the call. It had been a good night's work, and there was still time to grab a few hours of sleep before heading to his lab at the institute.

18

I took Rosie back to the Drakes Island house. Some breakfast for her, some more coffee for me, and then a walk on the beach. I wasn't sure what awaited me at MTRI, but I knew it wasn't going to be a good day. Bad news travels fast, and I suspected that word of Emily Weston's turn for the worse—if not her death—had preceded me. I could already hear Carlson yelling at me to stop the trial. But was that the right reaction to a single unexplained death? Mrs. Weston's unfortunate illness may have been a result of drug toxicity. But it also could have been something else. And stopping the trial prematurely had its own risk—that of depriving needy patients of a potentially lifesaving treatment. Not a decision I was prepared to make lightly.

It was too early for most people to be out, so Rosie and I had the beach to ourselves. Except for a flock of sandpipers, who were busy flitting in and out of the water like little windup toys, following the waves as they reached the shore and then receded back into the Atlantic. They moved in unison, confidently following an undesignated leader.

It would be nice if I could provide that kind of leadership to MTRI. I needed to somehow deal with Mrs. Weston's unfortunate death without letting any investigation get bogged down in the controversy that swirled around Carolyn. How to do that with a faculty dominated by Carlson and his cronies was less than straightforward.

Besides, there was something else bothering me about Mrs. Weston: her hair loss. As the nurse had said, hair loss was a common side effect of chemotherapy. But that applied to conventional chemotherapy, the kind of standard cancer treatments that killed not just cancer cells, but also many of the patient's normal cells. That lack of specificity was what made conventional chemotherapy so toxic, with hair loss being one of the most common and visible side effects.

But the new cancer treatments were different. They targeted specific proteins in cancer cells, like the RTKs, without the broad general toxicity of conventional chemotherapy. To be sure, targeted cancer treatments still had their toxic side effects. Diarrhea, nausea, and vomiting were the most common. And many patients experienced skin problems, like rashes and dry skin. But hair loss was not a common side effect of targeted therapies. Of course, who knew what the particular combination of drugs in Carolyn's trial might do?

I needed to do some background reading on the side effects of aloxinor and the other drugs she was using. And I wanted to find out if any of her other patients had experienced hair loss, or for that matter, anything like the respiratory complications that had killed Mrs. Weston.

As director, I could certainly pull and review the relevant patient records. But it wasn't my job to personally investigate this sort of problem. Like any other institution, MTRI had an Institutional Review Board—an IRB—that was responsible for reviewing and monitoring clinical trials. Which raised the question, who was on the IRB?

I stopped and sat on a large rock while I pulled out my phone and Googled the MTRI IRB. The home page had a link to the membership. To my chagrin, the chair was Tom Carlson. There were two members of the community on the board, both of whom were physicians. And then five additional MTRI faculty members—three of whom I remembered as having expressed opposition to Carolyn's promotion when I met with them last week.

There was no way that this committee would give Carolyn a fair hearing.

The MTRI faculty members on the committee, including the chair, served at my pleasure. Meaning that I could request their resignations and replace them with a more balanced group. But doing that was too heavy-handed. The resulting controversy—especially forcing Carlson out of an important administrative role—would leave the institute in flames.

Fortunately, there was another way. The time-honored ploy of academic leadership: *When in doubt, create a new committee.* In this case, it would be an ad hoc committee charged with investigating Emily Weston's death and transmitting their recommendation on continuation of Carolyn's trial directly to me. And it would have a membership that I could trust to be objective.

* * *

Anna looked surprised when I walked into the office at MTRI. "I thought you were going to be in Boston today."

"Bit of a change of plans. I'll be here for the rest of the week after all. Anything happening?"

"Just a call from Tom Carlson a bit earlier. I told him you were in Boston but that I'd let you know he wanted to reach you."

I wasn't surprised that Carlson was already after me. At least a call was better than having him show up unannounced.

"Could you get back to him and tell him that I'm here after all? And make an appointment for him later this morning, say eleven thirty. I have a couple of things I need to do first, but let him know that I'm anxious to speak with him as soon as I can."

Anna looked up with a raised eyebrow. "You're anxious to meet with Carlson?"

I smiled. "Yes. And be sure to tell him that."

Hopefully that would hold him until I had time to set my plan in motion.

* * *

Leslie Farnsworth was intently focused on her computer when I knocked on her office door. She looked surprised to see me. "Dr. Parker. Back for another chat? Is there something we didn't talk about before?"

I took a chair across from her desk and chose my words carefully. As an accomplished scientist, a member of the IRB, and the senior woman in the institute, she'd be perfect to chair my committee. Not to mention that she'd been supportive of Carolyn and dismissed Carlson as a chauvinist during our previous conversation. But chairing the committee I had in mind would put her in an uncomfortable political position in the institute. I had to present this in a way that would leave her knowing that I had her back.

"A problem's come up that I'd like to get your thoughts on. Can you spare a few minutes?"

"Let me guess," she said. "Carolyn Gelman's patient."

I nodded. "I take it that word's already spread."

She gestured toward her computer. "I was just reading an email from Carlson, calling for an emergency meeting of the IRB to investigate. He says the patient experienced severe toxicity and died in the ICU."

I wasn't surprised that Carlson was moving full speed ahead. "I'm afraid that's correct."

Farnsworth bowed her head for a moment. "How awful. I'm surprised to see that kind of toxicity with the drugs Gelman's using."

"At this point, we don't know whether the patient had a toxic reaction or not. Gelman says she's been in the trial for quite some time without any previous problems and was in remission. But we need to look into it and consider whether it's safe for the trial to continue."

"Carlson's already calling it severe drug toxicity. There's not much doubt what he'll recommend. And he dominates the IRB. Only I and one other member, Hank Richards, have been known to go against him. Which leaves him with a clear majority."

I nodded. "I understand. However, this is such an emergency that I don't want to wait for the normal IRB process. I've decided to appoint a small ad hoc committee to investigate it instead, charged with making a recommendation directly to me as fast as possible. I think that'll allow us to make the most expeditious response to the situation."

She looked up with a quizzical expression, her head tilted slightly to the right. "That's interesting. And do you have a plan for the membership?"

I ventured a hint of a smile. I suspected that she'd already figured out where this was going. "I'm thinking of just three faculty members to conduct an expedited process. And I'm hoping that you'll agree to serve as chair."

There was a light in her eyes that hadn't been there before. "This is such an important issue, how could I refuse? You do realize that Carlson will be furious."

I shrugged. "I'm meeting with him later this morning. I'll make sure that his anger's directed at me, not at you."

"I see. Well, it's your neck. Did you have anyone in mind for the other members?"

"You mentioned Hank Richards as another member of the IRB. Would he be good?" Richards was another one of the faculty members who I thought was at least moderately supportive of Carolyn.

Farnsworth smiled. "An excellent choice. And how about Carl Pollack for the third?"

Pollack had been on the fence about Carolyn when we spoke, but he was clearly willing to consider the case on its merits. Which was all I wanted.

"Fine with me. Do you want to ask them or should I?"

"I'm happy to—I'll go see them now." She got up. "And thank you. For giving us the chance to deal with this fairly."

"No, thank *you* for taking it on. I'll let you know once I've talked to Carlson, and you can move forward." I started to leave, and then I remembered. "Oh, one other thing I wanted to mention. I was at the hospital and saw the patient in the ICU last night. Her hair was falling out."

Farnsworth looked puzzled. "That's odd. Hair loss doesn't usually happen with these kinds of drugs. I'll be sure to look into it."

19

I got back to my office with just enough time to call Karen before Carlson was due to show up, so I shut myself in and dialed her number. It went to voice mail, meaning she was in a meeting or out on a case. I sent a text instead; she could read it at her leisure.

Things are crazy here. Carolyn's patient died last night. She's devastated. I wound up spending the night at her house because she didn't want to be alone. Husband was in Portland and wouldn't come home, seems like a real asshole. Have set up special committee to investigate patient's death, but will need to stay up here to manage things. Talk later. Xoxo

The knock on my door came as soon as I pressed send. As if it were on cue. I checked my watch—Carlson was right on time.

I arranged my face into a smile as I got up to greet him. No matter how much I disliked the man, my goal was to make this meeting as smooth as possible.

I greeted him with what I hoped passed for genuine warmth. "Thanks for coming to see me. Let's sit over here." I motioned him to my conference table, setting a more informal tone than our previous meetings when I'd made him sit in a chair across from my desk.

Carlson ignored my attempt at friendliness. "Gelman's case has become a very grave matter," he pronounced. "A toxic death like this in a clinical trial could compromise the reputation of the entire institute unless it's dealt with quickly and definitively."

"I couldn't agree more. Prompt and decisive action is clearly needed."

He looked momentarily surprised. "I'm glad you agree. I'll call a meeting of the IRB as soon as possible, hopefully within a couple of days. We'll need to review the records, and then we'll be able to order a halt to the trial. We need to get the community members involved, so the process may take a week or so. But I'll move as fast as I can."

"I think we need to move even more rapidly. I want to see this *resolved* as soon as possible."

"Absolutely, I couldn't agree more," he said. "The only problem is our community members, who have to be invited to all IRB meetings. They're very willing to help, but they're both physicians, and scheduling can be a little tricky."

I nodded sympathetically. "I understand. But evaluating this problem doesn't need full IRB involvement. I've decided to appoint a small ad hoc faculty committee to review the case and report directly to me for action. That should let us move with appropriate haste."

He smiled. "That's an excellent idea. I'll be happy to chair a streamlined committee to take care of this. Would you like me to find the additional members?"

"Thank you; I appreciate the offer. But I think having you as chair would make it look as if it were still the IRB, which would then be operating outside of regulations. I've asked Leslie Farnsworth to take the lead on this, and she reluctantly agreed. She's getting the other members on board now."

His eyes bulged as he sat up in his chair. "Farnsworth! You can't have her do this."

"Why not? She's the senior woman in the institute, so we won't face any accusations of gender bias. And she's a member of the IRB, so she's well versed in the necessary procedures."

"But she's a major supporter of Gelman! We can't trust her to handle this objectively."

I waved a hand. "Surely you don't mean that. An issue of patient safety—I think we can have full confidence in her objectivity."

He snorted. "I suppose the other members have been chosen as well?"

"Hank Richards and Carl Pollack."

He turned red as he stood and leaned over the table, thrusting his face into mine. "You son of a bitch, you think I don't know what you're trying to do! With that committee, you're turning this into a whitewash of Gelman."

I started to respond, but he cut me off. "Don't bother to deny it. The question is why? What's your relationship with her? Whatever your reason, I'm not going to let you get away with this."

He turned and walked out, without bothering to slam the door this time. Maybe he was set on more deliberate action.

I took a deep breath and went to my desk to send Leslie Farnsworth an email.

Just talked to Carlson. He's pissed of course, but all clear for you to proceed.

Her response was immediate.

Good, thanks. I've already talked to Richards and Pollack. They're on board. We need to get the trial records from Gelman. Should I go see her, or do you want to tell her what's going on first?

I responded that I'd talk to her and headed to Carolyn's office. The door was barely cracked open, so I knocked and waited.

The voice from inside was less than welcoming. "Who is it?"

I pushed the door open and went in. "Just me. How're you doing?"

Her expression morphed into a smile. "Oh, hi. I'm hanging in, trying to act as normal as possible. Thanks for stopping by."

I nodded my approval. "Actually, there's something I need to talk to you about."

Her smile faded. "I know, you're going to have to do an IRB investigation of Emily's death. I understand; you don't have any choice."

"We do need an investigation, but I've decided not to use the IRB. I've appointed a special ad hoc committee instead."

"Of course, whatever you think. Carlson will be chair, I assume. Who else will be on it?"

"Actually, Leslie Farnsworth will be chair. The other members are Hank Richards and Carl Pollack."

Her eyes widened. Then she grinned. "My God, thank you! Do you know what you've done?"

"No more than my job. This will ensure that the case gets prompt action." I gave her a wink. "And that you'll get a fair hearing."

I suspected that she was still smiling when I got back to my office. I certainly was. So far, it had been a good day's work.

But I knew there would be more to come.

20

With the crisis of Carolyn's patient at least temporarily on hold, I set up a Zoom meeting with the members of my lab back in Boston. It wasn't like being there, but it was a semi-decent substitute. Not only did it give us a chance to see and talk to each other, but it also let them show their data on the screen so we could look at it together as we discussed future experiments.

I'd gotten about halfway through my roster of lab members when my phone buzzed to announce an incoming text. I took a quick glance at what it was, and had to stifle a gasp of panicked surprise. Then I interrupted my Zoom meeting, saying an emergency had come up and I'd get back to them later.

My hands were shaking as I held the phone in front of me. The message was a photo of Carolyn and me on her front porch. She was wearing her robe and pajamas and had her arms wrapped around me in the hug she'd given me as I was leaving. The accompanying text was brief and to the point.

Hope you enjoyed yourself last night. But time to stop protecting her. Back off her case.

A mix of reactions ripped through me. First my stomach turned over. *How could someone do this to me?*

Then rage boiled up. *Carlson! I'll kill the son of a bitch.*

I tore out of my office and headed down the hall to Carlson's. He'd gone too far this time. I fantasized about beating him to a pulp, but rationality slowly began to take over. Even better, I'd use this to force him to resign. Attempting to blackmail me was unacceptable by any standards—I'd have his job for it.

It wasn't until I was halfway to his office that doubts began to surface. If I confronted Carlson with the text, he'd just deny that it was from him. Probably laugh at me for thinking he'd do something like that. I needed proof that he was the sender before I could act.

I stopped in the hallway and took a deep breath. Then I took my phone out to check the sender's number. No luck there. It was from the 213 area code, not Maine's 207.

Googling area code 213 told me it was from Los Angeles. Not obviously Carlson, but it could have been sent from a burner phone or a fake number. He was smart enough not to use his own phone for this.

I didn't know how to trace the number to get further information. But I knew who did.

I started back to my office to call Karen.

By the time I got there, two sets of questions were bouncing around in my head. First, was it really Carlson? Whoever took the picture had to have known I was at Carolyn's house last night and had been waiting there when I left this morning. I had trouble imagining Carlson pulling that off. Could he have a private investigator following Carolyn? Or me? Possible, but either of those alternatives seemed like a stretch. Why would he bother? He couldn't have anticipated this.

Getting Karen's help, with the resources of the FBI at her disposal, was undoubtedly the best way to sort this out. But did I really want to send her this picture? It wasn't exactly innocent-looking. Which of course was why the blackmailer had threatened me with it. True, I'd already told Karen that I'd spent the night at Carolyn's, but she hadn't responded to my message. I didn't know what she was thinking at this point, and if she was upset, this photo wouldn't help.

On the other hand, it would be better for her to get it from me than from whoever was trying to blackmail me. And after all we'd been through together, Karen and I knew each other about as well as any two people could. We trusted each other, and I could trust her with the truth of this. My fears to the contrary were paranoid. Right?

I forwarded her the text, with a brief explanation. And a queasy feeling that wouldn't quite leave the pit of my stomach.

This photo is crazy. Call me to talk about it. Someone took this when I was leaving Carolyn's this morning and is trying to blackmail me. Can you figure out who it's from?

The minutes passed slowly. I thought about reconnecting with the lab in Boston, but couldn't concentrate on anything else while I waited for Karen to call. Twenty minutes went by, and I was sweating. I looked at the photo again. Carolyn was wearing pajamas and a lightweight robe, clinging tightly to me. It didn't look like just a friendly hug. Had Karen misinterpreted it? Or rather, drawn the obvious conclusion?

Finally, she called.

"Want to tell me what the hell's going on?" Her voice was cold.

"Like I texted, Carolyn was upset about her patient going into the ICU last night. Her husband was in Portland, and she asked me to stay over so she wouldn't be alone. I spent the night in her guest room and left the next morning, when someone took that picture."

"So nothing happened? You were alone in the guest room all night?"

I wanted to say "Yes" and move on. But I couldn't.

"No, it got more complicated." I heard a sharp intake of breath on the other end of the line, but I continued. "The patient died in the early morning hours, and the doctor called Carolyn. She was hysterical and she came in, asking me to hold her. She spent the rest of the night in bed with me, but nothing else happened. I swear, we're not involved that way."

Silence on the other end of the phone. It felt like hours passed before Karen spoke.

"Shit, Brad. Do you really expect me to believe that?"

I broke into a sweat as I started to protest. "It's true—"

She cut me off. "Look, I can't deal with this now. Let's put it on hold and talk more about it when I see you. That is, if you still want me to come up on Friday?"

"Of course! Karen, I love you. There's nothing between Carolyn and me."

Her voice stayed cold. "All right, I'll see you Friday then. I need some time to try to process this."

My stomach turned over. "Karen, please. Nothing happened. Can't you trust me?"

"I'd like to," she said after a long pause. "I'll try. We'll talk Friday."

21

I stared at the wall after Karen ended the call, a hollow ball of fear in my stomach. How could I have been so goddamned stupid as to send her that photo? Of course she was upset; what had I expected? My eyes settled on the picture of piping plovers. An endangered species. Like my relationship with Karen had suddenly become.

My dark thoughts were interrupted by the ping of an incoming text. It was Karen! Had she realized things were okay between us? I opened the message in eager anticipation, only to be let down again.

I don't know what to feel or think about the photo. It will take time. But I wanted to let you know it came from a burner phone. My guys can't identify the sender, but they did track down where it was sent from by checking the phone's location. It was from Boston, the Kendall Square area in Cambridge.

At least she cared enough to try to help. Maybe things would be all right. I'd just have to respect her wishes and give her a few days. I didn't know how I'd manage that, but the best I could do was try to focus on something else.

Her text seemed to rule out Carlson as the culprit. He'd been in my office this morning—no way he could have sent the photo from Boston. Conceivably, he'd sent it to an accomplice there, who then sent it to me. But that seemed like far too intricate a plot for him to have set up. First having me tailed to Carolyn's, then an all-night stakeout to get the picture, now someone in Boston to act as a relay. As much as I wanted to think it was Carlson, I couldn't believe he'd put all that together.

Then who? Someone sneaking a picture like that smelled like a private investigator. Maybe someone was tailing Carolyn. Her marriage certainly didn't seem like it was in very good shape. Maybe her asshole husband was having her followed, hoping for divorce ammunition.

But why would her husband want to use the photo to make me back down from supporting her? It would be in his interest for her to get tenure and keep her job if he was planning on a divorce. Unless he just wanted to hurt her so badly that he didn't care about a potential divorce settlement.

I realized that I was getting nowhere when Anna knocked and came through the door. She had an odd look on her face—somewhere between surprise and awe. "It's President Houghton's office. They want me to get you on a Zoom conference with her."

I would've laughed at her expression if I wasn't too upset from my call with Karen.

"It's all right, Anna. She's president of the university, not the country. Just send me the link and let me know when."

"I just emailed you the link. They said it's an emergency and she's waiting to talk to you now."

I signed on and was greeted by the unsmiling face of Claire Houghton's receptionist. "Please hold, President Houghton will be with you shortly."

Moments later, Claire Houghton appeared on the screen. "You make enemies pretty quickly," she said. "Good ones, too."

Carlson? His complaining about me wasn't unexpected, although I was surprised by the apparent urgency of Claire's reaction.

"Can't say I'm surprised. Making enemies has always been one of my talents. Carlson?"

"Of course, Carlson. I've heard from him a couple of times, but he's easy enough to put off."

"Then what's the problem?"

"I got a call today from Arthur Friedland. He's not so easy to ignore."

The name rang a bell, but it was vague. "Who's he?"

She sighed audibly. "For one, he's a member of my board of trustees, and one of our biggest donors. Meaning when he talks, I listen. He's also a friend of Carlson's, and to make matters worse, he's one of the higher-ups at Pharmathor."

"The company that's sponsoring Mark Heller's aloxinor research?"

"Correct. As well as giving Carlson a hefty sum. And according to Friedland, you're endangering his company's investment at MTRI by allowing Carolyn Gelman's clinical trial to become a scandal."

"Oh, for Christ's sake! That's ridiculous."

"We don't tell Arthur Friedland that he's being ridiculous. He says that one of Gelman's patients has died of drug toxicity and the trial should be halted. But you've refused to do so. Friedland says that allowing this to continue will taint the institute's entire reputation."

"It's true that a patient has died, but there's no evidence that her death was due to drug toxicity. In fact, given the history of both the patient and the trial, I think that's highly unlikely. I've appointed a faculty committee to look into it, and I'll act according to their recommendation."

"Which is something else that Friedland complained about. He says you stacked the committee in Gelman's favor because you're committed to supporting her tenure case. Why isn't the IRB investigating this?"

"Because Carlson's chair of the IRB and he's determined to get Gelman kicked out. She wouldn't get a fair hearing from the IRB, so I appointed an independent committee that'll give her one."

"And what's your relationship with her? Why are you pushing to help her?"

"I'm just trying to do what you asked—to be sure that these tenure cases are properly handled. There's something strange going on with Gelman's case. A lot of the faculty are strongly set against her. They don't like her as a colleague, and several were openly hostile at her tenure seminar. Especially Carlson. She's been routinely badmouthed, and don't forget that someone attempted to sabotage her work by unplugging her freezer. And now she has to deal with the death of a patient, which is traumatic for anybody. All I'm trying to do is to make sure that she gets a fair shot."

"And do you have a more personal relationship with Gelman? What do you have to say about this?"

She held up a phone to the screen. With the picture of Carolyn and me from this morning. Whoever my blackmailer was, he was no slouch.

"Shit! They sent it to you already."

"I take it you've seen this before. Answer my question: Are you or are you not having an affair with Carolyn Gelman?"

"Absolutely not." I told her the story, just leaving out the part about Carolyn coming into my bed during the night.

She shook her head when I finished. "I'd like to believe you, but you've got to know that story's a stretch. You sure as hell can get yourself into some deep shit. For your sake, I hope they don't send it to Karen."

I tried to keep my face neutral. "I already did. I wanted to see if she could trace the sender."

She looked at me without saying anything for a long moment. Then she frowned and shook her head. "I hope she believes you. The best I can do is give you the benefit of the doubt for now."

I wished I knew whether Karen believed me. Maybe she, too, was just giving me the temporary benefit of the doubt. But I wasn't going to share those concerns with Claire Houghton.

"All right," I said. "I understand where you're coming from. But tell me, what phone number did your message come from?"

She checked and gave me the number.

"Mine came from the same phone. Karen said it's a burner, and her team couldn't identify the sender. She was able to tell that it was sent from the Boston area, though."

"Do you think it's from Carlson?"

"I don't know. That was my first thought, but he was here when the message to me was sent. Meaning that he'd need to have an accomplice in Boston, as well as having had someone stake out Gelman's house last night. As much as I'd like to believe it's him, all of that organization seems like a bit much."

"Well, whoever it was, the question remains what to do about it. Even if I believed your explanation, I can't ignore this. Not in the face of complaints from both Carlson and Friedland. I need to get you out of there."

"No. I need to finish this."

She leaned forward so that her face filled the screen. "What the hell do you mean, *no*? I just fired you."

"Look, something's really wrong here. A rumor mill targeting a junior faculty member, sabotage of her research, and now blackmail. All designed to force Carolyn Gelman out of her job. Why would anyone go to these lengths? Just give me enough time to figure this out. And fix it."

She glowered at me through the screen. "Goddammit. Why can't you ever keep things simple? How much time do you need?"

"Two weeks. I should have the committee's report on the patient's death in a matter of days. Once that's settled, I can go ahead and hold a faculty meeting to discuss and vote on the tenure cases. Both of them. Then I'll write up my director's report, and it'll be back to the university process. On its way to your desk."

"I'll give you until the end of next week, no more. Send me your letter of resignation immediately, effective end of business next Friday. That's the minimum time I need to get someone in your place anyway, so Friedland will just have to live with it."

She broke the Zoom connection, leaving me staring at a blank screen.

At least my time at MTRI would soon be over.

22

The call surprised him. Between the patient's death and the photo he'd sent the boss yesterday, he figured things would be done. But apparently not. Good. It would mean another hefty deposit into his off-shore bank account.

"Another patient needs to die," the boss said. "And quickly."

"Whatever you say. The photo wasn't enough for you to finish things?"

The boss's voice rose a notch. "Obviously not. Are you questioning my orders? Just do as you're told!"

The boss must be pushed to the edge to lose control like that, he thought. Fine. I can up my price.

"My apologies. Of course, I'm not questioning you. Just surprised."

The boss made a snorting sound, but his voice softened. "Good. Parker's apparently trying to whitewash Gelman, and he's been given until the end of next week to bring the case to a conclusion. We need another patient death before then."

"That much speed will be difficult."

"What's the problem? At the dose you're using, it only takes a day or two for the poison to work."

"The patients get a thirty-day supply of their drugs, so if I substitute one tablet in their bottles, it can easily be a few weeks before they take it. We were lucky with Weston; she only had three pills left when I visited her."

"So substitute all of their tablets with poison, not just one!" the boss shouted. "What the hell's the matter with you? Think!"

He held the phone away from his ear for the tirade. The boss was really losing it. Time to up the ante.

"That would be very risky. All the other pills would be left in the dead patient's bottle. They could be discovered easily."

"That's ridiculous. Nobody's going to run analysis on a dead patient's remaining pills. Just do it. Grow some balls."

He bristled at the insult. People didn't talk to him like that. It was lucky for the boss that he wasn't here. He was probably right that the risk was minimal, but the bastard would pay for his insolence.

"Have you forgotten our agreement? I decide how to do the job, and whether or not it's safe for me to proceed. I haven't succeeded in this business by taking unnecessary risks. If you don't like that, I'm sure you can find someone else who you think has bigger balls."

It was a bluff—the boss wouldn't have time to find anyone else. Not if he wanted this done immediately.

There was a brief pause on the line. "All right, I apologize. Would twice the normal fee persuade you to take on the additional risk?"

"Accepted. I'll get on it as soon as I confirm the usual fifty percent down payment has been transferred to my account."

The money was there when he checked five minutes later. The boss might be a bastard, but at least he was an efficient one.

He put on the brown UPS uniform and retrieved the bottle of white powder from his dresser drawer. Fixing a whole bottle full of pills would be a hassle, but worth it for the double pay.

23

I couldn't shake the feeling of unease as I waited for Karen to arrive. She said she'd leave by four, but Friday afternoon traffic out of Boston could be a bear. Everybody wanted to get out of the city for the weekend. She probably wouldn't get here until six at the earliest, maybe even seven. And here it was, barely five thirty, and I was sitting on the deck of our Drakes Island house with butterflies in my stomach. Like a nervous teenager.

It wasn't work. Leslie Farnsworth had called earlier in the afternoon to tell me that her committee had already completed their review. They found no evidence that Emily Weston's death had resulted from drug toxicity, and were recommending that Carolyn's trial be allowed to continue. She'd write up a full report over the weekend and have it for me first thing Monday morning. Which still left me the rest of next week to bring the tenure battle to conclusion.

No, it was the prospect of seeing Karen again that had me unnerved. Or maybe *terrified* was a better word. Did she believe that my relationship with Carolyn was professional? Friendly, to be sure, but not intimate. Or did she think we were lovers?

She said that she'd try to trust me. But we'd only exchanged a few brief texts since then, and I had no idea what she was thinking. Now I was about to find out.

Rosie heard the car first and went racing to the front door. I followed and started down the front porch stairs as Karen got out. She turned to me with a look that sent a chill down my spine. The wide-eyed look of a deer caught in headlights. Panicky and ready to run.

I went to kiss her, but she turned her face away. "We need to talk."

I followed her through the living room and out to the deck, where she sat in one of the Adirondack chairs in the corner.

"Do you want a drink?" I asked.

"No. Just sit down and talk to me."

She stared at me as I sat next to her. Without even a hint of a smile.

"Okay, where do you want to start?"

"Why don't you start by telling me again what happened the night you stayed at her house?"

"All right, but it's just what I already told you. There's nothing more. Do you really want me to repeat it all?"

"I know what you told me, but it's gotten all muddled up with that damned photo of the two of you. I want to believe you, but honestly, I'm confused. Just humor me and go through it again."

I went through the whole story, starting from when Carolyn called me to ask that I come to her house and leaving nothing out. Karen listened without any display of emotion. When I finished, she sighed and shook her head.

"Do you really expect me to believe that you spent the night in bed with this attractive young woman and didn't have sex?"

"That's what happened, so yes, I guess I do expect you to believe me. At least, I hope to God that you do. It's the truth, and you mean everything to me. Why do you call her attractive, anyway? Are you making something up about her in your head?"

"I checked her out on Facebook. She's young and sexy, no two ways about that. And in addition to spending the night with her, you seem obsessed with helping her get tenure. I just can't accept that there's nothing more to it."

"Karen, what can I say? She may look sexy in her Facebook pictures, but she was a sniveling mess when she got into bed with me that night. There was nothing attractive about her—it was like comforting a hurt child."

She shook her head. "If something did happen, just tell me. Please. I think I could forgive you, it's just this crazy doubt that's tearing me apart."

My head had started pounding. The truth obviously wasn't working, and I didn't know how to get through to her. "I can't tell you something that didn't happen. Can't you try to believe me? After all we've been through together?"

Tears started to form in her eyes. "I guess I'll have to try. Like you're some sexless knight in shining armor. I don't know if I can get past this, but I don't want to lose you. I'll try."

I got up to reach out to her, but my phone rang. I glanced at it to see who could be calling on a Friday evening.

Carolyn.

I answered with a curt "Yes?"

The distress in her voice was obvious. "Another patient is sick. Like Emily. I'm at the hospital. Please come."

"Oh Christ, I'm sorry. I can't come right now, but I'll try to get there later. I'll call you back."

"Okay, please come as soon as you can. This is awful."

I ended the call. Karen was looking at me expectantly. I rolled my eyes. "That was Carolyn. Another patient has gotten sick. She wants me to go to the hospital."

Karen nodded. "You should go."

"No, I'm not leaving you in the middle of this."

She gave me a weak smile. "I'm trying to believe you, remember? And if I do, you have a friend asking for your help." She got up. "I'll go with you. Maybe seeing the two of you together will help me understand."

24

Neither of us said much during the ride to the hospital. When we got there, Carolyn was sitting in the ER waiting room. I thought it was the same chair that she'd been in the first time I met her here. Next to the bubbling fish tank.

She looked up when she heard us come in. Her face was red and tear-stained. "Thanks for coming," she sniffled.

I sat down next to her and started to take her hand, but hesitated. Then I looked at Karen. Her face had softened into an expression of concern.

I put my hand on Carolyn's shoulder. "I'm so sorry. What's going on?"

"I don't know. It's…it's like with Emily. He complained of nausea and vomiting, and he's having trouble breathing. The doctors are in with him now."

She looked up at Karen. "This is my partner, Karen Richmond," I said. "We were at the house when you called."

"Oh, I'm sorry," Carolyn said. "I didn't mean to interrupt."

Karen came forward and took a chair next to Carolyn. "It's nothing, don't worry about it. Is there anything I can get you? A glass of water or some coffee?"

Karen's face was filled with sympathy. The rancor she'd shown on our deck seemed a thing of the past.

Carolyn managed a weak attempt at a smile. "No, I'm fine. My husband's coming soon. Just sit with me, please."

"How long has the patient been in your trial?" I asked.

"About four months. He's never had any problems before this. And he was fine when I saw him for a routine exam a week ago." She closed her eyes and shook her head. "It's a nightmare, like Emily Weston all over again."

Just then a figure in blue scrubs emerged from the ER. It was the same doctor we'd seen before, Dr. Ashland. Her expression was serious as she addressed Carolyn. "I'm afraid he's not doing well. We're going to take him to critical care, but you can see him first if you'd like."

Carolyn nodded and got up. Ashland turned to me. "Dr. Parker, I remember you from before. You're welcome to come, too." Then she looked quizzically at Karen.

"This is my partner, Karen Richmond. Can she join us?"

Ashland shrugged. "Why not?"

We followed her to a room toward the back of the ER. A man with long gray hair was in the bed with an attendant beside him. He was on oxygen and hooked up to a monitor that displayed heart rate, blood pressure, oxygen saturation, and other vital signs. Carolyn rushed to his side, while Karen and I stayed a step behind.

The patient looked at her blankly as Carolyn tried to talk to him. "Mr. Reed, it's Dr. Gelman. I'm so sorry this is happening. Don't worry, everything's going to be all right. I promise."

She stroked Reed's head gently. He made a soft moaning sound as a clump of hair fell out and rested on his pillow. Maybe it was some vague kind of recognition, but I didn't think he knew what was happening.

Carolyn tried to say something else, but her voice broke and she turned away. Tears were running down her face, and she threw herself hysterically into my arms. "My God, they're all dying! I'm killing my patients!"

I tried to hold her away and looked at Karen anxiously. This was like pouring gasoline on the fire of her suspicions. But her face radiated sympathy, not anger, and she returned my look with a faint nod.

With a sense of relief, I took Carolyn into my arms as she sobbed for what seemed like several minutes. Then Dr. Ashland said, "They're here to take him up to critical care. I'll be in touch as soon as we know anything more."

I supported Carolyn, who was still crying hysterically, with an arm around her waist as the three of us made our way slowly out of the ER suite. When we reached the waiting area, a tall brawny-looking man dressed in a fashionably tailored gray suit and red silk tie was pacing the floor. His face turned a color that matched the tie when he saw us.

"What the hell are you doing with my wife?"

So this was Carolyn's husband. I already had him pegged as a jerk, and he was certainly living up to the image. I wanted to tell him to go screw himself, but I kept my cool.

"I'm sorry; she's just upset about her patient. I'm Brad Parker. I take it you're Carolyn's husband."

His eyes bulged and he turned even redder. "Get your hands off her! Are you screwing her, you fucker?"

He drew back a massive fist to take a swing at me, but Carolyn jumped in front of me and grabbed his arm. "Stop it, Paul! He's just helping me with my patient."

That drew his fire to Carolyn. "You whore!" he screamed, shoving her so that she staggered backwards into one of the chairs that lined the side of the room.

He turned back to me and raised his fist again. I'd dealt with bullies like this before, and I was relishing the idea of knocking him on his ass. But Karen stepped in and shoved her badge in his face. "All right, that's enough. Calm down. I don't want to have to arrest you."

Instead of complying, he spat out, "Fuck you, bitch!" and took a roundhouse swing at her. Karen sidestepped it, grabbed his arm, and twisted it behind his back. When he struggled, she gave it a hard yank, which elicited an abrupt cry.

"Now you've attempted to assault a federal officer, asshole. Do you want to stop or go to jail?"

He again tried to twist away, and Karen yanked upward on the arm. This time he screamed with the pain. "Aargh, let go! You're breaking my arm!"

"Not yet. But I can certainly break it if you want me to. Or are you ready to cool it?" She gave the captive arm another yank to drive the point home.

I could see tears as he groaned in pain. He ceased his struggles. "All right, stop. Please."

"When I let you go, I want you to sit down and keep yourself under control while we talk. Are you ready?"

He nodded and she led him to a chair across from Carolyn. He sat docilely, looking subdued and fearful. A bully brought to heel.

"I'd enjoy throwing your ass in jail, but I really don't want to waste any more of my time on you," Karen said. "So I'll settle for apologies."

"Thank you, officer. I'm sorry I lost it."

Karen nodded. "And to your wife."

That was clearly harder for him. He glared at Karen and then turned to Carolyn, anger still in his eyes. "I'm sorry, honey. I shouldn't have shoved you."

"It's all right," Carolyn said. "I know what a strain this is on you. But really, there's nothing going on between me and Brad."

"No, there isn't," I interjected. "You must realize how hard this is for Carolyn."

He nodded. "I do. Again, I'm sorry I lost my temper."

The change was too quick for me to believe. But Karen said, "Okay. Are you in control of yourself now?"

He nodded again.

"All right," Karen said. "You're free to go if you want to."

"Why don't you go ahead home?" Carolyn suggested. "I'll follow soon and pick up the kids on my way. That'll give you a chance to relax for a bit."

We sat quietly with Carolyn for several minutes after he left. Then Karen asked, "Will you be all right tonight if you go home?"

Carolyn's eyes were sad when she answered. "Yes, it'll be fine. He just gets this way sometimes; he has a bad temper. Probably from his father. He'll be over it by the time I get home."

We stayed a few more minutes before Carolyn thanked us profusely for coming, assured us that she was all right, and said we could go. I was hesitant to leave her, but I sensed that she needed some time by herself before going home to deal with whatever awaited her there. I told her to call if she needed anything or if there was any news. Then Karen and I took our leave.

When we reached the reception desk, I noticed the woman who had been there on my last visit was back on duty. She recognized me and smiled sadly. "I'm so sorry you're here with someone else again. It's the same kind of thing, isn't it, and now it's happened to two patients from your institute. So sad. Funny, this patient also has a Russian relative. A cousin from Los Angeles called to check on Mr. Reed, and he has a Russian accent, just like poor Mrs. Weston's brother."

Two patients whose relatives had Russian accents? There was nothing funny about it. I knew what Karen would say to a coincidence like that.

25

By the time we left the hospital, though, I had more on my mind than Russian accents. I wasn't sure what to expect from Karen at this point. How had she interpreted Carolyn falling into my arms when we saw the patient? And her husband's accusation that we were having sex? If things between us had been bad before, I feared they'd be even worse now. Going home might be no better for me than it was going to be for Carolyn.

I got into the car and looked over at Karen as she sat in the passenger seat, trying to read her thoughts. Instead, she read mine.

"It's okay, Brad." She leaned over and cuddled against me. "I understand now. Seeing her made it clear. That poor woman."

I put my arm around her as an enormous wave of relief flowed through me. "So you saw what it was like for me that night?"

"Yes. She's like a puppy in distress. Of course, you did your best to comfort her. I would've done the same—anyone would have. At least anyone decent."

"Anyone except that brute of a husband."

She shook her head. "What an asshole. Do you think she'll be all right with him tonight? Should we drop by and check on her?"

"I'm afraid that would only make matters worse. She probably knows how to handle him by now."

"I suppose you're right. Brad, I'm so sorry. I should have trusted you and believed you from the beginning."

"It's all right. That damned photo of Carolyn and me together made it hard, not to mention my telling you that she spent the night in bed with me. Should I have left that out?"

I started the car and began to back out of the parking space.

"No, you were right to tell me. It shows you trusted me enough to be honest about what happened. And I should have had that kind of confidence in you." She ran her hand up the inside of my thigh and smiled coquettishly. "Maybe there's some way I can make it up to you."

"Maybe there is," I said, as her hand reached my growing erection.

She giggled. "Hold that thought while you get us home."

We drove in contented silence as I navigated through the side streets to US 1 and turned north toward Drakes Island. I was happy to bask in the relief of a crisis averted, but Karen's mind was—as always—still churning.

"Do you think he's seen the photo? He went after you like he had, but he didn't say anything about it."

"I was wondering the same thing. In fact, I'd been thinking earlier that it could have been taken by a private detective he had following Carolyn. But I don't think that's it now. He would have been screaming about it back there if he'd seen it."

I glanced over to see her nod and purse her lips. "Who are you thinking then? Carlson?"

"That would make sense. And it would fit with it being sent to Claire Houghton."

"Oh! I didn't know she'd seen it."

"Yes. She got me on Zoom to grill me about it. Said both Carlson and one of his buddies who's on the board of trustees were after my ass. She wants me out of here, although in the end, she gave me another week to finish things up."

"You've really been bombarded with this crap." She reached over and squeezed my arm. "I'm sorry; I should have been here for you. Not making things worse."

"Don't worry about it. This was hard on both of us, and I'm just glad you're here now. I'm not sure about Carlson, though. He couldn't have sent the text from Boston, he was in my office that morning. Plus, the whole thing seems too intricate for him to have pulled off."

"He could have hired someone, though. Whoever it was must have been following you, and they're clearly a pro. They had to be prepared to do an all-night stakeout and take pictures the next morning."

"That sounds crazy. It's way over the top to try and get me to drop my support of Carolyn's tenure case. I've seen academics do some pretty weird things, but this is hard to swallow. Even for Carlson."

Karen started to say something, but then interrupted herself to stick her arm in front of my face and yell, "Hold it! Pull into the left here!"

I moved over to the left-turn lane and hit the brakes. Maybe she'd spotted someone tailing us. But she gave me a somewhat sheepish grin and pointed across the road. "We're stopping at that lobster place. I remember it from last summer. They have cooked lobsters there that we can take home."

I couldn't stop laughing as I pulled into the lobster farm. "What's so funny?" Karen asked. "We have to eat. This way we'll be all set to have lobsters in bed."

"No argument; sounds like a perfect plan." I parked and got two pound-and-a-quarter lobsters, which were apparently so popular during the summer months that they always had them cooked and ready to go.

My mind was racing ahead to being home in bed with Karen by the time I got back to the car, but she'd returned to thinking about whoever was blackmailing me.

"Did you notice anything strange that night you spent at Carolyn's? Maybe somebody unusual at the hospital while the two of you were there?"

"Afraid not. The only people we talked to at the hospital were Dr. Ashland and the woman at the reception desk."

"The same woman who was there tonight?"

"Yes. Friendly lady."

"What was she saying about the first patient's brother? He had a Russian accent, like Mr. Reed's cousin who called tonight?"

"That's what she said. And it seems more than a little weird. The first patient's brother was there that night, but he was already on his way out when the receptionist pointed him out, and I couldn't catch him."

"Did you get a look at him?"

"Just from the rear, before he got into his car. Blond hair, well built but short. Maybe around your height."

"Hmm, interesting," she said. "So, both patients have relatives with Russian accents, and one is short and well built."

I looked over and saw that her eyes had lit up. "It certainly seems suspicious. What are you thinking?"

"Short Russian men have been on my mind lately. You remember that mob hit in Boston, the one that kept me late the night you told me about the job up here?" I nodded and she continued. "We don't have much, but we did get the shooter on video. Can't see his face, but he's short. The analysts put him at about five-six. And the victims were Russian mob, so our assumption is that the shooter is, too."

"You're thinking there's some connection to what's happening up here? That seems awfully thin."

"I know, but there's another video of a five-foot-six-inch mystery man."

Suddenly it hit me. "Right! The asshole that unplugged Carolyn's freezer."

"And the patient's brother you saw at the hospital? The one with a Russian accent. You said he was about my height, or shorter. I'm five-seven, which puts him in the same range. So that makes three."

"Okay, I agree that that's a lot of short Russian men. But there's nothing to tie any of this together, is there?"

We'd reached Drakes Island Road, so I made a right off of Route 1 and headed for home. My thoughts were turning to Karen, bed, and lobsters. In that order. Happily, leaving the highway seemed to have a similar effect on Karen.

She put her hand back on the inside of my thigh. "I don't know, but something about all this is raising my hackles. Too much coincidence. But for now, why don't you get us home? I think our lobsters are ready for bed."

26

I woke to find Karen snuggled tightly beside me with her head on my shoulder. It was tempting to stay like that, but it took only a few minutes for Rosie to realize that I was awake and start pawing me. So I carefully extricated myself without waking Karen and headed downstairs. Coffee for me and out to the yard for Rosie.

It was gray and misty with enough wind to drive the ocean into a froth of waves crashing into the shore. A bit chilly, but a nice show to watch as I sat on the deck with my coffee and skimmed the night's emails on my iPad. Nothing noteworthy in my inbox, which was just as well because Karen came down in a few minutes, clad in nothing but a light robe that came down no further than mid-thigh. A tantalizing enough picture to reawaken my ardor from last night.

I got up to give her a kiss, which started to develop into something more, but she stopped me with a grin and a wink. "Hang on, I need some coffee. And then we have some work to do."

"Ah, always work. What's so urgent?"

"Don't worry, there'll be time for more fun and games later. But first I want to check out these supposed relatives with Russian accents."

That brought me fully back to the seriousness of Carolyn's situation. I had no choice but to call an immediate halt to her drug trial, even while the second patient's sudden illness was being investigated. A second patient that I hoped was still alive.

"Yes, that'd be good to do. And I think I'd better call Carolyn. I want to find out about her patient, and I also have to give her the bad news about her trial."

"And don't forget to find out how she is," Karen reminded me. "I wasn't entirely happy to let her go home with that animal last night."

I rolled my eyes as I dialed Carolyn's number. She picked up on the third ring. After affirming that she was okay, she told me that the patient—Mr. Reed—was still in intensive care, but stable and conscious. She was on her way to the hospital and had pulled off the road to take my call.

I would have liked to put off delivering my next message, but there was really nothing to do but spit it out. "I'm glad to hear that. Keep me informed when you see how he is. In the meantime, I'm afraid there's something else we have to talk about."

"My drug trial?" Her voice was trembling. "I understand. You have to stop it, don't you?"

"I'm sorry, but yes. With a second patient suddenly ill, I don't have any choice. At least until we know what's going on."

"I can't believe we're seeing this kind of toxicity without any previous indications of a problem. But I understand, there's nothing else you can do. I know how supportive you've been."

I felt like crap when we ended the call. Neither of us mentioned it, but we both knew that whatever chance she had at getting tenure was rapidly going down the tubes. And I couldn't put a final vote off past the end of next week.

Karen had gone down to the beach with Rosie while I was talking to Carolyn, so I went ahead and did the necessary dirty work. First, I called Leslie Farnsworth and brought her up to date with instructions to add Fred Reed's case to her committee's investigation. She was horrified at the illness of a second patient, but almost as surprised as Carolyn had been. Nonetheless, she agreed that stopping the trial was the only option at this point.

I had to take a deep breath before making my next call. But I needed to let Tom Carlson know. As chair of the IRB, it was up to him to implement a halt to Carolyn's trial. I prepared to eat crow as I punched in his number.

His response to the news was pretty much what I expected. "About time you decided to do your damn job. I'll have the IRB order an immediate stop to her trial."

The glee in his voice was obvious. So much so that I couldn't let it stand. "Hopefully it'll just be a temporary measure while Leslie Farnsworth's committee has time to look into this second case. It still doesn't seem like drug toxicity to me."

"You've got to be kidding," Carlson said. "It's as plain as the nose on your face. I'm looking forward to the faculty vote on Friday, when we can get rid of that worthless bitch once and for all."

After ending the call to Carlson, I went down to join Karen and Rosie on the beach. Rosie was running in and out of the water, chasing the waves as they crashed into the shore and then receded back into the ocean.

It didn't take Karen long to divine my mood. "What's wrong? You look like you'd like to strangle someone."

"Carlson. The bastard can't wait to put the screws to Carolyn."

"How'd *he* find out?"

"I had to call him. As chair of the IRB, he's the one to officially put a stop on Carolyn's trial. Now he can't wait until Friday, when the faculty's scheduled to vote on her case."

"Can't you delay the vote until you figure out what's happened?"

"Not really. Claire Houghton insisted that Friday's to be my last day at MTRI. Besides, it seems pretty obvious, doesn't it? Two similar cases has to mean drug toxicity."

She looked at me shrewdly. "You don't really believe that, do you?"

I sighed. "In my gut, no. But in my head, what else is there to think?"

"There's too much else going on," Karen said. "Lab sabotage, blackmail, and strange men with Russian accents."

"So you think what? Carolyn's somehow being set up with this? I can't believe that her patients are being murdered just to prevent her from getting tenure."

"I agree, that seems too flimsy a motive. But something smells wrong. And it sounds like we have one week to figure it out before your faculty vote."

A wave of gratitude swept over me. Karen had reversed course since yesterday. She was now completely on Carolyn's side. And on mine. Maybe with her help we had a shot.

"Meaning you're going to help with this? Don't you have to get back to Boston?"

"I already let the office know that I'd be spending the week up here to follow a new lead on the Russian mob killing." She smiled and shrugged. "Who knows? Maybe that's what I'll be doing."

"So where do we start? Do you want to talk further with Carolyn? She said she was going back to the hospital."

"Maybe later," Karen said. "First I want to track down the first patient's brother. The one who supposedly lives in Sanford and you saw in the parking lot."

"You want to see if the brother's a short guy with a Russian accent?"

"Yep."

"Sounds good. I should be able to get his address from the MTRI patient database."

"Get the info on Fred Reed's cousin, too, while you're at it."

"Why? Are we going to make a trip out west?"

"No, but I'll have someone in the Los Angeles office check him out while we visit Sanford."

27

Sanford was only half an hour from Drakes Island, but it felt like a world away. Whereas Wells had one of the lowest crime rates in Maine, Sanford had one of the highest. And it turned out that Emily Weston's brother lived in the worst part of town, near town center. When I gave Karen the address, she laughed, saying it was a haven for drug dealers and it would be interesting to meet this mysterious brother.

As we neared our destination, I started to feel like we were back in one of the rough areas of Boston. There was no landscaping, just houses packed together on small lots with uncut lawns. Almost all were badly in need of painting, and most had obvious areas of rotted wood and sagging gutters. A few of the more run-down ones had broken windows to complete the picture.

The address we had for Emily's brother—Charles North—corresponded to a run-down three-story New England–style house that looked like it might be a multifamily. There was only one door, though, so we made our way carefully up the rotting steps and rang the bell. No answer, and the bell hadn't made a sound, so I tried knocking instead. That got us a grudging shout to wait a damn minute. Eventually, the door was opened by a pudgy red-haired woman wearing a ratty-looking T-shirt and black sweatpants. She stared at us with bleary eyes until Karen broke the silence.

"We're looking for Charles North. Is he here?"

"He don't live here."

"I'm sorry to bother you then, but we have this as his address," Karen said. "Do you have any idea where we might find him?"

The woman stamped her foot. "That asshole, he ain't supposed to give this as his address. He's just one of our renters—go knock on the side door. Goddamned son of a bitch." Her cursing trailed off as she turned away and slammed the door on us.

"One of their renters," I said, as we walked around the house. "How many people do you think live in this pit?"

"You don't want to know," Karen replied. "Looks like this is the side door."

The stairs here were even worse than in the front of the house, but we made it up safely and I knocked. No answer, so I tried again, louder.

"All right, damn you. I'm coming, I'm coming."

The door was opened by a tall thin man with unfocused brown eyes. He looked us up and down with evident hostility. "What do you want? You look like some kinda fuckin' cops."

Karen showed her badge. "I'm with the FBI, but there's no problem. We just need to ask you a couple of questions. Are you Charles North?"

"What if I am? Is it any business of yours?"

"Look, we can either do this the easy way or the hard way. Easy is you identify yourself and answer a couple of questions. Hard way is we make a trip to the local cop house and question you there. Your choice."

"All right, I'm Charles North." He pronounced it *Chahles Nawth* with a thick Maine accent.

"Emily Weston's brother?"

"Ayup." A glimpse of interest showed in his eyes. "Why, the old cow leave me some money when she croaked?"

"We don't know about her will," Karen said. "But we're wondering if you visited her in the hospital the day she passed away?"

He spat to the side of my foot. "Ain't seen that sorry bitch in years. You want anything else?"

We made our way back to the car without falling through the stairs. "Well, that was fun," I said. "Great place to visit."

Karen shrugged. "I've been in worse places. At least we learned what we needed to know."

"Yes, he's a tall Mainer. Not a short Russian."

"Yep." She pulled out her phone. "Hang on a minute, I've got a text from my colleague in LA." She paused for a moment. "Okay, that's clear enough. The cousin is in a nursing home with Alzheimer's. He couldn't have called the hospital if he wanted to, with or without a Russian accent."

"So neither of the calls or visits were legitimate. From either Emily Weston's brother or Fred Reed's cousin."

"Correct. I think we can presume that both were from the short guy you saw in the hospital parking lot. And that he has a Russian accent."

"Meaning there's some sort of mystery man who's checking on Carolyn's sick patients?"

Karen nodded. "And I'll bet he's the one who followed you to Carolyn's house from the hospital, staked it out, and took the picture."

"As well as being the asshole who sabotaged Carolyn's freezer. But all we know is that he's short and has a Russian accent. How do we find the prick?"

My phone buzzed with the ring of an incoming call before Karen could answer. It was Carolyn. "Brad, I'm at the hospital. Mr.

Reed is awake and he just told me something important about his medication. He thinks he may have made a mistake with the dose. I think you should talk to him, too."

"I'm in Sanford; be there as soon as I can. Maybe half an hour."

My heart started beating faster. Could this be the explanation? I filled Karen in as we headed to York Hospital.

28

There was a different woman at the front desk than the one I'd talked to on my previous visits. But she was equally pleasant and promptly phoned the doctor to come and get us. It was only a few minutes before a tall, youngish man in a white coat and a navy-blue tie came into the lobby.

"Dr. Ashland's off today," he explained. "I'm Dr. Dworkin. Please come with me."

We started to follow him, but he stopped when he saw Karen. "I'm sorry, just Dr. Parker, if you don't mind. I don't want too many people crowding my patient."

Karen took out her badge. "I'm with the FBI. Special Agent Richmond. This is part of an active investigation, and I need to hear what your patient has to say. Directly from him."

Dworkin scowled and looked as if he were going to object, but Karen's expression apparently changed his mind. He grunted in acquiescence and led us to the ICU. I'd guess he was one of those men who didn't like women in positions of authority.

Carolyn was sitting next to the patient's bed. He was awake, but still hooked up to oxygen, an IV, and monitors that beeped irregularly in the background. Overall, I didn't think he looked much better than he had the day before. Although maybe just being awake was a good sign.

Karen and I went over to stand next to Carolyn. She took the patient's hand. "Mr. Reed, this is Dr. Parker. He's the director of my institute. Can you tell him what you told me before about your medicine?"

He turned his head laboriously in my direction and looked at me with eyes that were half glazed over. "I…I may have taken two pills. Made myself sick."

"I'm so sorry you're ill, sir. But it's going to be all right. Everyone's working to make you better." I wished I believed my own words. He looked like he was barely hanging on, not at all like he was going to be all right. "Why do you think you took a double dose?"

He managed a weak smile. "My memory's not always so good, so I have a system. I turn the bottle every night so that the label is on the left. Then the next day when I take the pill, I turn it to put the label on the right. That way I know I've taken it for the day. I don't forget."

His voice was becoming weaker and he stopped talking to concentrate on taking in some oxygen. Dr. Dworkin started over, presumably to stop us, but Karen held up her hand.

"That's a good system," I said. "But why do you think you took two in one day?"

He breathed in deeply and rallied. "It was the day before I started getting sick. I came home in the afternoon and went to take my pill, as usual. But the label was on the right, as if I'd already taken it for the day. I was confused. I usually take them in the afternoon, and I didn't think I'd taken one that morning. So I figured that I'd probably forgotten to turn the label to the left the night before. I didn't want to miss a dose, so I took another one. But now I think maybe I messed up and I really *had* taken one that morning." His breathing was labored and he stopped talking to concentrate on his oxygen.

"I think that's enough," Dworkin said, and started to motion us out. But Karen stopped him again.

"Just one more thing," she said. "Mr. Reed, do you mind if we go to your house and check out the pills? We can tell if you took too many by counting how many are left in the bottle."

He managed a weak "Okay." Then his eyes closed and his head rolled to the side. I noticed another clump of hair had fallen onto his pillow as Dr. Dworkin swooped in and chased us out of the room.

* * *

Like Charles North, Fred Reed lived in a rental unit in a multifamily. But the similarity ended there. Reed lived in an attractive neighborhood in York, just a few minutes from the hospital. When we reached his address, we found a freshly painted two-story Colonial right across the street from the beach. We parked on the street and walked up a flagstone path to the front door, which had a directory identifying Mr. Reed's unit.

Karen had gotten the key from one of the attendants at the hospital, so we let ourselves in without difficulty. The apartment was comfortably furnished with gleaming hardwood floors and a blue-and-white patterned area rug in the living room. There were two bedrooms, one of which apparently doubled as an office and a guest room. The bottle of pills was next to the sink in the single bathroom.

"The label's on the left," Karen immediately noted. "I think we can take that to mean he didn't take one yesterday before he got sick and went to the hospital."

"I agree. In which case, his last dose would have been Thursday, when he thinks he may have taken two."

She picked up the bottle and examined the label. "Looks like this was filled on the twelfth. With a total of thirty tablets."

"Okay, today's the twenty-fifth, which makes Thursday the twenty-third. Let's assume he took his first pill from the bottle the day after he got it, which would be the thirteenth." I used my fingers to count the days. "That would mean he should have taken eleven."

Karen repeated my count. "Okay, I get the same number. So, there should be nineteen left, right?" She emptied the bottle and started counting. When she finished she frowned. "Wait, I want to check it again." After the recount, she looked up and shook her head. "Nineteen it is. He didn't take a double dose."

I wasn't so sure. "If our assumptions are correct, that is. What if he had an old pill left and didn't start this bottle until the fourteenth?"

"Yes, that would screw things up," Karen agreed. "And be consistent with his having taken two when he got sick. Unfortunately, I don't know how we're going to figure that out."

"About the only thing I can think of doing is asking him and hoping that he'll remember. Carolyn's probably still at the hospital, should I ask her to do it?"

Karen nodded. "I'm not sure we'll be able to trust his memory of ten days ago. But sure, give it a try."

It took four rings for Carolyn to answer her phone. When she did, she explained that she was on her way home and had to pull off the highway to take my call. Her husband had gotten angry at her absence and insisted that she come home to give the kids their lunch. But she planned to go back to the hospital later that afternoon and would try to ask Mr. Reed then.

I disconnected and gave Karen the news. In the meantime, she'd put the pills back in their bottle.

"So, we're done here?" I asked.

"Yeah, let's go get some lunch ourselves." She picked up the pills and put them in her pocket.

"What are you doing with those?" I asked.

"I'm going to send them to the lab and have them tested."

Tested. I was puzzled. "Why? What are you looking for?"

"I don't know; just call it a cop's intuition. We're wondering if the patient accidentally gave himself an overdose. Why not also make sure there's not some mistake in the pills themselves? Maybe the pharmacy made them up at the wrong dose. That could explain both of the patients getting sick, right?"

I smiled appreciatively. "Good idea, it wouldn't be the first time cancer patients have gotten accidental overdoses. I remember back in the nineties, two patients got a huge overdose of chemo at one of the major hospitals in Boston. One of them died and it was a big mess. Do you want me to have the pills checked out at the MTRI pharmacy lab?"

"Sure, go ahead. But I'm going to send some to the Bureau's lab as well. Just in case somebody at MTRI might try to cover up their mistake."

29

The call came as a surprise. The second patient was in the hospital. Maybe not dead yet, but sick enough to be in the ICU. So what now?

"We've got a problem," the boss said. "That damned Parker and his FBI girlfriend. They picked up the remaining pills from the bottle you doctored and they're having them analyzed to be sure they're the right formulation."

"Shit! Those are all poison. I substituted the whole bottle. Like you told me to, dammit!"

"I know, I know. Take it easy, you can fix it. The bottle's in the MTRI pharmacy. Parker just dropped it off there late yesterday. They're planning on doing the analysis tomorrow."

"So you're thinking I can go in and switch them back? How about I just grab the first plane back home and leave you holding the bag? This is your damned fault. I told you it was stupid to substitute the whole bottle."

The boss's voice turned to ice. "That would be a mistake on your part. Don't forget that I have friends back home. Remember how I found you in the first place?"

Yes, he remembered. Through the chief of one of the most brutal gangs in the Russian Mafia. A man it wouldn't do to cross.

"Sorry, I didn't mean anything. You just caught me by surprise. Yes, I can get in and switch them back. I'll let you know when it's done."

* * *

Security at MTRI had tightened after the bastard Parker took over as director. There was now a guard at the door after hours, so he decided against making another night raid. Instead he went to the institute in the late afternoon, waved to the security guard, and went up to his desk in the lab. He'd pretend to work for an hour or so until the pharmacy closed at five. Then he'd pay them a visit.

At five thirty he took the back stairs down to the first floor. The pharmacy was dark, and he used his master key to quietly slip in. Unnoticed by the guard sitting at the door reading a magazine.

He had to hunt around for several minutes before he found the bottle of pills. It was in an out-tray on the pharmacist's desk with a note saying, "For analysis first thing Monday." Clearly labeled as a prescription for Fred Reed from Dr. C. Gelman.

Finding the correct pills was easier. There was a stock bottle on the dispensary shelf labeled "C. Gelman, clinical trial."

Good; now just to make the switch. He opened the bottle waiting to be tested. One look and his heart started beating rapidly. There were only ten pills in the bottle. Just two days ago, he'd filled it with twice that number.

He put the ten in his pocket for later disposal and replaced them with ten from the legitimate stock bottle. Then he returned both bottles to their original locations and left, waving again to the security guard on his way out. But the satisfaction of a job well done eluded him. Instead, he felt a mounting sense of danger.

Where the hell were the rest of the poison tablets?

* * *

It didn't take the boss long to return his call after he left the message at the emergency number.

"Is it done?"

"Not quite. I'm afraid we have a problem."

"What problem? Can't you just get your job done right?"

He held the phone away from his face for a moment. He wasn't going to let anybody talk to him like this. Like he was a child or an idiot. Powerful friends or not, he'd make the boss pay for this.

"The pills that Parker left at the pharmacy are gone, substituted with the real thing. There was no difficulty with the job. But there were only ten pills in the bottle. There should have been twice that number."

The boss was silent for a moment. Then he said, "So you're worried that Parker still has the rest? And will do something with them?"

"Yes, that's my concern."

"But if the analysis from the pharmacy comes back clean, what more would he do? I don't think we need to worry about this."

"I disagree. It's a loose end, and I don't like loose ends. Not when it's my neck sticking out."

Another pause on the line. Then, "Maybe you're right. What do you propose?"

"You don't need to know. Don't worry, I'll take care of Parker and his FBI girlfriend at no additional charge. The cleanup will be my pleasure."

30

Monday passed slowly. First I heard from Carolyn. Mr. Reed had been asleep when she visited Saturday afternoon and again on Sunday. But she'd finally been able to catch him when he was awake this morning and ask if he remembered whether he'd started using his last batch of meds the day after he'd picked them up. His memory was clear. He'd taken the last pill in the previous bottle that afternoon and then had to rush to the pharmacy before it closed in order to get his refill for the next day. So yes, he was sure that he'd started the new bottle the day after he picked it up. Which pretty much ruled out the possibility that he'd accidentally overdosed himself by taking two pills the day before he got sick.

That bit of bad news left me anxiously waiting to hear from the pharmacist, hoping that Karen had guessed right and there'd been an error in compounding the prescription. It was late afternoon before her email came in.

Per your request, I've analyzed Mr. Reed's tablets by mass spectrometry. I'm pleased to report that their composition is precisely as ordered. We made no error in compounding the prescription.

Please let me know if I can be of any further service.

So much for my hopes that something was wrong with the pills. I couldn't concentrate on anything else, so I packed up and went home. Maybe Karen's day had been more productive.

* * *

She was on the deck, reading something on her Kindle, when I got there. I told her my news.

"Too bad," she said. "I'm still waiting to hear from the Bureau's lab, we'll see if they get the same results. Actually, I'm surprised it's taking them so long, especially if the pills are nothing other than what they're supposed to be. Anyway, something else happened today that I wanted to ask you about. Did you know the gas man was coming for a service check?"

"No. What gas man?"

"You didn't authorize a service visit? I took Rosie down to the beach an hour or so ago, and when we got back a guy was coming up from the basement. He apologized for surprising me, but said he thought we knew he was coming. When nobody was home, he used his key from the rental company to come in and do the annual inspection of our heating system. Everything was fine, he said."

"Okay, doesn't seem like a big deal."

"Probably not. But let's call the rental agency and see if they know about it. His uniform was from Atlas Oil."

I made the call and asked if we'd been scheduled to receive a service visit from Atlas Oil. The woman on the other end said to hold on and she'd check. She sounded concerned when she came back on the line.

"You're in the Drakes Island house, right? We have strict instructions not to authorize service visits without your permission, so

I'm sure we didn't set this up. And we don't use Atlas Oil at your address, either. Your house is handled by Lyman and Sons."

I assured the woman that there must be some mistake on our end and turned to Karen. She was already placing a call on her phone.

"Grab Rosie and let's get out of here," she said. "I'm calling the Bureau to get a bomb team sent in and check out the basement."

A shock wave hit me. *The bomb squad.* "You're really worried?"

She looked at me as if I was a bit slow. "The supposed service man was well-built and a little shorter than me. Don't you think it's worth checking out? I probably should have reacted more strongly at the time, but he mumbled so I couldn't tell about an accent, and he had long scraggly red hair rather than blond hair like the guy you saw in the parking lot. But it could have been a wig."

Two black SUVs sped in, blue lights flashing, less than twenty minutes later. Four men and a German shepherd got out. Three of them started putting on bomb suits while the one with the dog came over to us. He introduced himself as Captain Bookman, the squad leader, while his dog and Rosie sniffed each other.

"Any idea where we should concentrate our search?" Bookman asked.

"He was coming up from the basement when I got home and surprised him," Karen said.

"Okay, we'll start there. I need you folks to keep away from the house. Why don't you go wait down on the beach?"

Bookman donned his gear and the four men went into the house, the dog pulling at the leash in her eagerness to get to work. They emerged half an hour later carrying something in a metal box, which they put in a larger box in the back of one of the SUVs. That done, Bookman motioned us back up from the beach.

"It didn't take Elsa very long to sniff it out," he said. "What a nose on that girl!" He gave Elsa a pat on the head as she and Rosie resumed their sniffing routine. Then he turned serious. "Damn good thing you called us. It was a detonating device, tied into your gas line and set to go off at two in the morning. It would have taken out the whole house and would have looked like some kind of freak accident."

My knees were shaking. *Someone had just tried to kill us.*

But Karen seemed to absorb this calmly. "I'm not surprised," she said. "Thank you for dealing with it so quickly. I'll get a forensic unit over to look for prints or DNA, but I doubt they'll find anything. He was wearing gloves when I saw him."

"Worth a try; you can never tell. In the meantime, I think the two of you should stay somewhere else tonight, just in case we missed something." He looked at Rosie. "Sorry, I should have said the three of you. There's plenty of motels around that take dogs." He patted Elsa again, and then bent down to pet Rosie. "At least little ones like your girl."

31

Karen remained calm while we got everything into the car and I drove off in search of a motel. How she did it was beyond me. The idea that we were the intended targets of some kind of Russian assassin gave me the willies.

"I'm going to call and arrange for a sketch artist to meet us when we find a motel," she said. "Keep your eyes open for a place that's dog-friendly and looks clean."

I still wasn't thinking clearly. "A sketch artist?" I asked.

Karen shrugged. "May as well give it a try. I got a pretty decent look at him, and a good sketch might help give us an ID. He could even be in the Bureau's facial recognition database."

Once I turned onto US 1, motel possibilities popped up. Except most of them had No Vacancy signs lit up in front, which wasn't a surprise for the height of Maine's tourist season. We were almost to Ogunquit before I spotted a medium-size complex that not only said Vacancy but also had a Pets Welcome sign.

"How's this?" I asked. "Not that we seem to have a lot of options."

"Perfect," Karen said. "There's even a pizza place where we can get some dinner across the street. Go check us in while I call and give the sketch artist our location."

Half an hour later, we were in a comfortable if not luxurious room eating a pepperoni pizza with a bottle of white zinfandel that

I'd scored at a Cumberland Farms next to the pizza place. The pizza was cheesy and good, and Rosie gave it a high rating for the pieces of crust Karen kept giving her as treats. An almost relaxed domestic scene until we were interrupted by a knock on the door.

I got up to answer, but Karen stopped me. "Wait a minute." She went to her travel bag and took out a gun. "Just in case," she said. "I wish I'd had this handy when I ran into the phony service man. Go ahead, you can open the door now."

Our visitor was a rail-thin woman in her thirties with big round glasses and long red hair. She didn't seem surprised to be greeted by a gun pointed at her chest, simply showing Karen her ID and introducing herself as Patty Sullivan, the sketch artist. Then she gratefully accepted a slice of pizza, passed on a glass of wine, and got to work with Karen at a desk under the window.

It was interesting to watch. Most law enforcement agencies now used computer-based systems to generate facial composites, but the FBI maintained that hand-drawn sketches were more accurate. Patty began by asking Karen for a general description of the intruder. Karen being Karen, she systematically supplied plenty of detail—hair, mustache, glasses, shape of the suspect's face, mouth, nose, and so forth. Patty drew a preliminary sketch and asked Karen what needed tweaking. After a couple of rounds of adjustments, Patty dug into her bag and pulled out a thick book of photos. She went through them page by page, asking Karen to point out ones with a nose similar to the suspect's. Then the same for eyes, mouth, chin, and what seemed like a long list of additional features. The whole process took a couple of hours until Patty seemed satisfied and Karen sat back and said, "That's him."

I went over and took a look at the finished product. Patty seemed disappointed when I said I didn't recognize him, although

Karen didn't look surprised. "I didn't get much of a look at him, just from the back," I explained. "And he had long blond hair, not the scraggly red mess you have on this guy."

"Could have been a disguise," Patty said. "Let me do a blond version."

She made some quick changes and showed it to me again. I couldn't really tell.

"Could be," I said. "The hair's right now, but I didn't see enough of him to help."

"That's okay," Karen said. "I'll send both versions to the Bureau and they can run them through facial recognition. Maybe we'll get lucky."

It was almost midnight by the time Patty left. Karen took photos of the sketches, composed an email, and sent them off. The answer came back quickly. But I could see Karen's initial look of excitement fade to disappointment as she read the email.

"The system came up with two matches," she said. "Unfortunately, one died in a traffic accident last year, and the other's serving twenty years in federal prison."

"So that's it? There must be something more you can do with the sketch."

She shrugged. "I'll try circulating it to the local cops. Maybe they'll get a lucky break."

Then her phone buzzed again. "Hang on, this looks like something from the lab. Could be some results on the pills."

I watched as she opened the email. Then her eyes widened and her jaw fell. "Holy shit! It's thallium!"

"Thallium? What are you talking about?"

"The pills. They're thallium, not Carolyn's drugs. Someone's poisoned her patients!"

I was lost. "Slow down a second. What's thallium?"

"You've never heard of thallium? God, it's a classic poison. It was widely used in the fifties and earlier when it was readily available as a rat poison. Agatha Christie wrote a book about it, *The Pale Horse*, and it became known as 'The Poisoner's Poison.' Then its use was banned in this country in the seventies and it became hard to get. It's not readily available anymore, but it still crops up sometimes. It was a favorite of Saddam Hussein's, and there was a case in New Jersey a few years ago where a woman in a pharmaceutical company had access to it and poisoned her husband. And you know the major characteristic of thallium poisoning? The victim's hair falls out."

"Christ, just like what happened to Carolyn's two patients."

"Indeed. Get Carolyn on the phone right away. She has to get Mr. Reed on the antidote immediately."

It took several rings before Carolyn answered in a voice that was groggy from sleep. I put the phone on speaker.

"Carolyn, I'm sorry to wake you, but this is urgent. We're on speaker and Karen's here with me. She had some of Mr. Reed's pills analyzed, and your patients have been poisoned with a compound called thallium."

"Oh my God! Like in the Agatha Christie book?"

Despite the tension, Karen gave me a wink. "Yes, exactly," she said. "Get blood and urine tests on Mr. Reed, and get him started immediately on hemodialysis and Prussian blue."

"What's Prussian blue?" Carolyn asked.

"It's the only known antidote. It'll help clear the thallium from his circulation. It's not easy to find, but they'll have it in Boston somewhere. Maybe try Mass General."

"All right, I'm on it. Christ, this is crazy! Are you sure? How'd you figure this out?"

I stepped back in. "Carolyn, there isn't time to go through everything now. I'll fill you in as soon as we have a chance, but you have to take care of Mr. Reed right away."

"Yes, of course. I will."

"Good," Karen said. "And one more thing. Keep this to yourself, except for whoever you need to tell at York Hospital. Brad and I are starting to figure out who's responsible, but we don't have him in custody yet. And he's dangerous. For your own safety, I don't want anyone to know that you're aware of what's happening."

32

My mind was spinning after we ended the call to Carolyn. We now had a sketch of the short man with a Russian accent who'd poisoned Carolyn's patients and tried to blow up Karen and me. But that didn't give us an ID. Were we really close to getting him?

"Do you think circulating the sketch to local cops will work?" I asked.

Karen shrugged. "It's possible. That's how they got Timothy McVeigh, the Oklahoma bomber. But I'm afraid it's a longshot. We know that he disguised himself with the wig, and who knows what else he may have done. If he's good, the face I saw could only vaguely resemble reality. Even if an alert cop stumbles across him, he may not be recognizable."

That didn't give me a great sense of optimism. "So now what? Do you think he'll come after us again?"

"He might, it's hard to know. We need to get him before he has that chance." She looked at me with fire in her eyes. "And not just him. Our short Russian is somebody's hired gun. I want the bastard who's giving the orders, too."

"So how do we find him if the sketch doesn't do it?"

"Maybe there's another way. Who knew you took Mr. Reed's pills to the pharmacy for analysis?"

"Just Liz Shanbrun, the pharmacist. I emailed her and requested the analysis shortly before I dropped them off Saturday afternoon. Why?"

"Because the pills you dropped off must have been thallium, just like the ones I sent to the Bureau. But the analysis from the MTRI pharmacy came back as the correct prescription."

"Meaning you think Liz faked the analysis? I guess that's possible, but it seems unlikely. I remember her record: She was a pharmacist at Maine Medical Center for more than twenty years before coming to MTRI. Stellar recommendations."

Karen shook her head. "I actually don't think she's the most likely suspect. There's another possibility."

My brain was finally starting to get over the shock of learning about thallium and beginning to function again. "That our short Russian killer broke into the pharmacy and switched the poison tablets for real ones? But how would he have known I brought them in for analysis in the first place?"

She gave me a cynical half smile. "Want to bet your email's been hacked?"

"Oh shit, not again!" My email had been hacked a year ago by a spy in the lab at Harvard where I was doing my sabbatical. That had started us on a hunt that ended with Karen and me making a narrow escape from the clutches of a serial killer. It looked like we were well on our way to a similar mess—if not already there.

"Just a hunch. Open up your email and let's check your login history."

I signed in and handed her my laptop. "I have no idea how to do that, but I assume you do."

"Yep." She fiddled for a moment. "Interesting. Most of the logins are from just two IP addresses, which I assume are yours. But there seem to be a couple every day or so from odd addresses. Including one on Sunday morning."

"Meaning someone's hacking in?"

"Looks like. And they would have seen the email you sent to the pharmacist about dropping off the pills."

"Crap. So you're thinking someone broke into the pharmacy and switched the pills, leaving the correct prescription for analysis?"

"Mmm-hmm. And maybe that'll give us another lead on him. Is there still a security camera at the entrance to the institute?"

"There is. I posted a guard there too, trying to tighten up security after I came on as director."

"Can you access the video feed from here? Let's see if we can spot our short friend visiting MTRI on Sunday."

"Okay." I checked my watch. "But it's late, after midnight. Do you want to get some sleep and start on the video in the morning?"

"I'm not exactly sleepy, are you? Besides, time's running out for us to get him."

"How so?"

She looked at me as if I were stupid. Which I guess wasn't unjustified.

"By morning he'll know that we didn't go up in a firebomb. Then he'll either be after us again or, more likely, vanished into the wind."

I nodded and took my laptop back from her to pull up the video feed. "Let's watch a movie."

The video of the MTRI entrance was as boring as you could get, especially since we were viewing it at high speed and could just see people flitting in and out. But two hours into it, I caught a glimpse of our target.

I grabbed Karen's arm. "Hold it, I think that's him!"

She reversed the feed a bit and ran it again at normal speed. A short man with closely trimmed black hair entered the building and waved to the security guard. At that moment, the camera caught his face.

"Is that who you saw?" I asked.

She studied the image on the video. "It could be. If I imagine the hair different, and no glasses. Yes, I think that's him."

I checked the time stamp on the video. "He went to MTRI just after four on Sunday afternoon."

"Perfect timing to swap the pills," Karen said. "Let's see how long he stayed."

We started the video up again, no longer bored. It wasn't long before we saw the man come back in frame. Karen slowed it up, and we watched him exit, again waving to the guard, at five forty-eight.

"What time does the pharmacy close?" Karen asked.

"On Sunday? I think it closes at five."

"Figures. Looks like he got there an hour early and hung around until after it closed. Then he went in, swapped the pills, and left."

"How would he get in? The pharmacy must be locked," I said.

Karen looked at me with a raised eyebrow. "You don't think a hired hitman would know how to pick a lock?"

I gave her a slightly embarrassed grin. "I suppose he would. Although maybe he's gotten his hands on a key. He must work at the institute."

"Because of the way he just strolled in and waved to the guard? Yes, I was thinking that, too."

"Not only that; I bet he's on the scientific staff. Administrators or facilities people don't generally come in on Sunday afternoons, but scientists often do."

That earned me a smile. "Good point. Nice work, Watson. I don't suppose you have pictures of the institute scientists anywhere?"

"Oh, I think we do, Sherlock. All of the labs have websites with photos of their staff."

I navigated to the MTRI homepage and clicked on the heading Research. A list of the institute's research groups came up, and I clicked on the first name, Adams. That took me to the Adams Lab site, which had photos of eight lab members. Karen just shook her head. Nobody familiar.

I repeated the process for the Becker lab, the Bradley lab, and then the Carlson lab.

"That's him," Karen said.

I clicked on the picture to pull up a biosketch. "It says he's a visiting scientist in Carlson's lab. The name's Sergei Turgenev. The website says he got a PhD from Moscow University three years ago."

"Both the name and the PhD are probably fake. Can you send me the photograph? I'll pass that on to the Bureau. It'll have a better chance than the sketch of bringing something up from their database."

It didn't take long before her phone beeped with the tone of an incoming text. She looked at it and gave me a thumbs-up. "The photo worked."

She took a few minutes to read the message. Her expression was somber when she looked up.

"Hired gun is what he is, all right. A real pro. He's in the CIA database, known to them as former Russian intelligence, now freelancing as an assassin for hire. Apparently very good at his job, too. They think he's carried out several hits for the Russian mob, as well as being credited with two newsworthy political assassinations that were ordered by the state in his previous life. His real name's Alexei

Orlov, last spotted a year ago in Moscow. No record of his having entered this country recently, so he presumably got in as Turgenev or some other fake identity."

"So Carlson brought in a Russian hitman to work for him. That son of a bitch. But do you think Carlson knows who he really is? As much as I'd like to hang this whole thing on him, I have a hard time picturing Carlson using a hired killer to do his dirty work."

"Maybe not, but that's certainly what it looks like. I'm going to have them picked up, and we'll see when we question them. Can you get their home addresses?"

"Sure, they'll be in the personnel directory. You want both Carlson's and Turgenev's? Or I guess I should say Orlov's."

"Yes, I want to get them both in custody ASAP. Carlson's complicit in this mess, even if you're right and he's not running the operation. I'll send teams to their homes as soon as you give me the coordinates." She looked at her watch. "It's four in the morning. With any luck, they'll be asleep and we'll take them by surprise."

Karen went to the bathroom while I dug out the home addresses. I felt a welcome sense of relief. Soon Karen would have Orlov in custody. Carlson, too, and she'd figure out what was going on. This lunatic nightmare would be over.

Then the door flew open and someone burst into the room. With a jolt, I realized it was Orlov.

A black pistol with a silencer was in his right hand. Pointed at my midsection.

33

The blood drained from my face as a wave of shock and panic washed over me. My reaction seemed to amuse Orlov. He closed the door behind him and smiled. The way a cat would smile if it were about to eat a cornered mouse. "Good evening, Professor. You seem surprised to see me."

All I could think of was trying to stall. At least Karen was out of sight, behind the bathroom door. If I could let her know what was going on, maybe she could get out through a window. If there was one.

I spoke loudly, hoping she would hear. "Orlov! What are you doing here?"

"Ah, you know my name. You're better than I thought you'd be. Or your FBI girlfriend is. Where is she, by the way?"

Perhaps a display of more knowledge would slow him down. And distract him from Karen. "Yes, we know who you are. Or would you prefer that I call you Dr. Turgenev?"

He laughed coldly. "Actually, my name is now Kuznetsov." He took a passport out of his pocket. "It says so right here, and this is the passport I'll use to get back home. But you know a lot. It's good that I'm visiting you before I leave. Turn around and put your hands behind you."

"Fuck you!" I screamed to make sure Karen would hear.

He reacted by slashing the gun across my head, knocking me onto the bed. While I was too dazed to react, he grabbed my hands and used a plastic tie to secure them to the bedpost.

"There, that should keep you out of trouble. I was watching the house on Drakes Island. When two o'clock came and there was no fire, I knew something was wrong and it was time for me to get out. But I need to know how much you've uncovered first. And more important, who else you've told." He shrugged. "It might affect my travel plans."

I tried to clear my head. I couldn't think of anything to do besides stalling. Keeping him talking was the best shot. "How'd you find us?"

"You used your own credit card to check in here. Not too bright, Professor. An amateur move."

I cursed myself. Karen wouldn't have made that mistake.

He pressed the gun into my kneecap. "Now tell me what you know."

I figured there was no harm in that. "We know you're a Russian hitman and that you poisoned Carolyn Gelman's patients with thallium. And that you're here working for Tom Carlson. Your picture's been sent out to the cops already. They're out looking for you."

He smiled again. A cruel expression that sent a chill down my spine. "Thank you. I appreciate the information. Even if you're lying about the cops. Do you think I don't monitor police communications? But anyway, where is your girlfriend? I'd like to talk to her, too."

"She not here. She left a few minutes before you came. Heading to the local police station to arrange for your arrest."

Suddenly the shower came on in the bathroom. *Christ, hadn't Karen heard what was happening?*

Orlov chuckled. "I don't think so, it sounds to me like she's taking a shower. I'll just go and see."

I strained against the bedpost as he went to the bathroom. To no avail. I tried to yell out a warning, but he shoved a sock into my mouth. Helpless, I watched him throw open the door and step in, gun in hand.

Suddenly there was an ear-splitting scream. But it didn't sound like Karen. Then the room filled with the stench of burning flesh and Orlov staggered out. Karen followed, with Orlov's gun in one hand and a red-hot iron in the other.

She pushed Orlov, still moaning, to the ground and smashed the iron into the back of his head. He was silent after that, and she retrieved handcuffs from her travel bag. Once Orlov was secured, she cut the plastic ties that bound my hands.

"That should hold the bastard," she said. "Thanks for keeping him talking long enough for me to get ready. Handy that this place had an iron in the bathroom. You gave me enough time to get it heated up, and I was all set to smash it into him when he came through the door."

Orlov was still writhing on the floor, obviously in extreme pain. "Is he going to be all right? Should we call a doctor or something?"

She laughed mirthlessly. "Who gives a shit? I suspect he'll have third-degree burns, probably some broken ribs. But he'll live." She reached for her phone. "I'll call the local cops. They'll patch him up enough for us to question him."

Four Wells cops, two state troopers, and an EMT team in an ambulance showed up a few minutes later. The EMTs gave him a painkiller and put a dressing on his burns. At least the painkiller made him stop moaning.

"We're going to take him to York Hospital," one of the EMTs said. "He'll be okay, but they'll need to bandage him up and treat his wounds."

"Will I be able to question him?" Karen asked.

"I think so. Give it half an hour or so."

The Wells cops followed the ambulance to the hospital. The state troopers stayed behind and took our statements before we headed out after them. Back to York Hospital, which was fast becoming my home away from home.

Orlov was securely shackled to a bed in the ER when we got there, conscious though looking a bit rough around the edges. The expression on his face changed when he saw Karen. He didn't say anything, just stared at her with an odd look. Maybe respect. Or awe.

His voice was weak when he finally spoke. "How you do this to me?" He made a vain attempt to smile. "You must be good. Or maybe just very lucky this time?"

Karen ignored the bizarre compliment. "You won't have another time," she said. "Your killing days are over. Not much for you to look forward to now except life in a cage. We've got you for the murder of one of our patients, attempted murder of a second, and who knows what else we can dig up."

He tried to shrug, but that was apparently too painful to pull off.

"You might help yourself by talking to us. Who gives you orders? Carlson? We know he brought you here as a visiting scientist."

Orlov almost laughed, except the facial movement produced a jolt of pain instead. "Carlson? You must be joking. He's nothing. A fool we used."

That pretty much fit my assessment of Carlson, but I kept quiet.

"Then who?" Karen asked. "This is your chance to talk. Get yourself a better deal. Who's in charge of this shit show?"

He snorted his disdain. "I'm a dead man if I talk. Your prison won't protect me."

"Give me the man on top and I'll get you in witness protection. You'll be a free man with a new life ahead of you. Otherwise you rot in jail."

He was quiet for a moment. Then he said, "The boss is a prick. I don't mind if I give him to you." He gave her a sly look. "But can you authorize witness protection? I don't just take your word. I want a signed deal from the US Attorney. Get me that, then I tell you what I know."

"I'm a senior FBI officer, asshole. If I say witness protection, you'll have witness protection. But fine. I'll be back with someone from the US Attorney's office and a written offer tomorrow." She gave him a hard look. "Only what you have to say better be good. If not, I'll throw you in a goddamned cage myself."

34

He drifted in and out of sleep, the woman never leaving his thoughts. How could she do this to him? Take his gun away, burn him, beat him, put him in a hospital bed in shackles. When she was armed with nothing but an iron.

He'd killed many men when the odds were against him. Now, while he had his gun in his hand, this woman had broken him like he was nothing. A stick of wood.

She was special. Too good for the FBI. Far too good for that lame professor.

The kind of woman he wanted for himself. The kind of woman who deserved him.

35

Karen called the US Attorney in Boston as soon as we managed to get out of bed and inhale enough coffee to start functioning the next morning. Which wasn't until nearly ten, after what had been less than three hours of sleep. He agreed to the offer of witness protection, promising to send someone to meet her with an agreement they could present to Orlov later that day. In the meantime, we decided we had enough energy to pay Tom Carlson a visit.

He was in his office with two of his students when we got there. I knocked and we let ourselves in without waiting for an invitation. Carlson's response was predictable.

"What do you want? Can't you see I'm busy? Get out and make an appointment with my admin."

Karen held up her badge. "You need to talk to us now."

Carlson's eyes widened and the students looked confused. "The two of you can leave," I said.

The students got up and made a quick exit. But that gave Carlson time to regain his bluster. "Again, what do you want? You can't just come busting into my office."

"This is me being nice and giving you a chance to talk here," Karen said. "Do you want me to drag you down to the police station in handcuffs instead?"

Carlson's mouth moved, but nothing came out. Maybe he was starting to realize that playing the bully wasn't going to do the trick.

"Do you know Sergei Turgenev?" I asked.

"Of course, he's one of my visiting scientists. A good man, chemistry PhD from Moscow State University."

"How is he in the lab?" I asked. "Seem to know his stuff?"

Carlson fidgeted in his chair. "Well, he's only been here a few months. And I give people in my lab a lot of freedom, so I really haven't had much contact with him."

Meaning that Carlson didn't have a clue about whether Orlov/Turgenev knew any science or not. Sadly, that was probably true for pretty much everyone in his bloated laboratory.

"How'd you find him?" I asked. "Or did he find you?"

"I'm always open to good people who want to join my team. Turgenev wrote to me saying that he had a fellowship from Russia to pursue two years of research abroad. He was familiar with my work and said that he very much wanted to study next-generation cancer therapeutics. I asked him to provide references, which he did. They were glowing, so that was that." He smiled at me. "Always happy to attract a talented young scientist."

"Who were his letters of recommendation from?"

"His PhD advisor and two other faculty members at Moscow State. It's one of the most prestigious universities in Russia."

"And you contacted those people directly?" Karen asked.

Something in her tone took the edge off of Carlson's cockiness. "No, I have too many applicants to do that. I always ask the candidate to have his references write to me."

"They sent you emails? I assume from their university accounts?"

"Yes, of course. Glowing, as I said. Do you want to see them?"

Karen shook her head contemptuously. "Not really. They're nothing but fakes. Don't you realize how easy it is to concoct a fraudulent recommendation email?"

"You did nothing to check their legitimacy?" I added. "Or Turgenev's?"

Carlson was finally starting to look worried. "Well, no. I mean, these guys are all well-known scientists. And Turgenev knew what he was talking about—he even sent me a copy of his fellowship proposal."

That was enough for Karen. "You damned fool. The man you call Turgenev is actually a hitman for the Russian mob. His real name is Alexei Orlov, and he's responsible for poisoning two of the patients in Carolyn Gelman's drug trial. One of whom has died. We arrested him last night."

Carlson jumped out of his chair. He was trembling and leaned on the edge of his desk to brace himself. "That's insane! Poisoning patients! What the hell are you talking about?"

Karen held up a pair of handcuffs. "Turn around and put your hands behind your back. I'm placing you under arrest."

"For what? I don't know anything about this. You can't arrest me!"

"Conspiracy to commit murder. Hands behind your back."

"At the very least, you brought Orlov here," I added. "And you've been intent on destroying Gelman's career. It's hard to avoid the conclusion that you're directing his operation."

Carlson still didn't move, so Karen grabbed his right arm and slapped the cuffs on. When he realized what was happening, he went limp.

"I don't know anything about what he's done. You're making a mistake. Please don't do this. It's not my fault."

"It'll be up to the US Attorney to decide what's your fault or not," Karen said. "At worst, you're the mastermind of a murderous conspiracy. At the very least, you've let a killer slip into the country with fake credentials that you signed off on in his visa application. Either way, you have a lot to answer for."

36

As enjoyable as it was to watch Karen manhandle Carlson into the back of her car, it was probably no more than a guilty pleasure. I really didn't think he was responsible for anything more than gross stupidity. Which, for a man in his position, was probably enough to justify a night or two in jail, so the spectacle of his arrest was okay by me.

"Do you really think he's behind all this?" I asked Karen, once she had him secured in the backseat.

"Not really, no. I think he's a pompous fool that Orlov and his real boss manipulated. But who knows? Maybe we can get more out of him in interrogation. You don't feel sorry for him, do you?"

I shook my head. "No, not at all. If nothing else, his negligent, incompetent lab management brought Orlov to us. I'm going to see that he's finished here, once you're done with him."

"Good. Do you want to come to the cop shop with us?"

"Sure, if you want. I'm happy to ride along and make sure he doesn't give you any trouble."

She laughed. "That's sweet, but I think I can handle a buffoon like this."

"Yes, I'm sure you can." The thought of Carlson trying to attack Karen was laughable. "Orlov would probably agree with you, too."

I added. Then I paused and thought about my next moves. "If you don't mind, I think I'll stay here then. I need to get a couple of things taken care of in order to get the heat off of Carolyn."

She looked at me sharply. "Like what? Be careful not to let anyone know about the poison. We need to keep that to ourselves until we figure out who's running things. It's the only advantage we have at this point."

"I'm glad you said something. I was going to tell Leslie Farnsworth the story and have her get Carolyn's trial started again."

"Well don't," Karen said quickly.

I held up my hand. "I hear you, don't worry. But the secret's already out, isn't it? I told Carolyn last night, and now Carlson knows, too. He'll spread it all over the institute."

"Carlson won't be a problem. I'm going to make sure he's locked up tight and not allowed to communicate with anyone on the outside. And we already told Carolyn not to tell anybody. If you see her, maybe you should remind her of that."

"Okay, will do. Although I don't think she'll be a problem. There's nobody she talks to at the institute anyway."

Karen nodded. "Good. An assistant US attorney is planning to meet me at York Hospital at two to interview Orlov. Why don't you join us for that? Your perspective might help unravel whatever we manage to get out of him."

* * *

Oddly, Anna had a message from Leslie Farnsworth when I got to my office. She wanted to talk to me about something she'd noticed while reviewing the records of Carolyn's patients. I headed down to her office, where I found her at her computer, drinking coffee from an oversize ceramic mug emblazoned with the MTRI insignia and a black-capped chickadee, Maine's state bird.

"You were looking for me?"

"Yes, thanks for coming down. I just wanted to touch base on the Gelman situation. We looked into Fred Reed's record. It was just like Weston's. He had no earlier problems, nothing to indicate there would be a complication."

I wished that I could tell her the truth. But Karen had been adamant. "Good to know. But still, with two patients down, I don't see any alternative to stopping Gelman's trial."

She nodded. "Yes, that's clearly what you have to do. Is there anything else my committee can do to help?"

"No. At this point, I think you've done your job. Thanks for the quick work."

"Of course. There's something else I wanted to tell you, though. Something I noticed when I was going over the records of Carolyn's patients."

My heart fell. "What? Is there some new kind of problem?"

"Not toxicity, no. But the response rates of some patients seem off. She has two groups of patients, right? One group gets aloxinor while the second gets retoramib, one of the other RTK inhibitors approved for lung cancer. And then they both get the additional drugs she's hoping will combat the development of resistance."

I was anxious for her to get to the point. "Right, that's how I understand the study design. And?"

"Well, the response rates of the patients getting retoramib are nearly seventy percent, which is what's been reported. But only about half the patients in the aloxinor group seem to have responded to the treatment."

"That's weird. Aloxinor is supposed to be even more effective than other inhibitors, isn't it?"

"Correct. Approximately eighty percent response is what Carlson reported to the IRB when we approved the drug. And that's similar to what Heller subsequently published." She frowned. "I don't know…I guess this could be a fluke of small numbers. I was going to ask Carolyn about it at some point, but given the nature of my committee's investigation, it didn't seem appropriate for me to discuss it with her."

37

Carolyn wasn't in her office, but I found her when I got to York Hospital at one forty-five, sitting in the waiting room chatting with Karen and drinking coffees in Styrofoam cups. Any resentment Karen had harbored toward her was apparently a thing of the past.

I gave Karen a kiss and took a seat next to her. "How's the patient?" I asked Carolyn.

She shrugged. "No better, but he's stable. They started hemodialysis as soon as I gave them the news last night. Prussian blue is on its way, should be here this afternoon." She managed a weak smile. "At least there's some hope now."

"We'll just have to keep our fingers crossed," I said. "Did Karen tell you about Carlson?"

Carolyn nodded. "Incredible. He's in jail? Do you really think he's behind all this?"

"We don't know," Karen said. "But we're going to find out. Seeing what that bastard Orlov has to say when the AUSA—assistant US attorney—shows up will be a big step."

"At the very least, Carlson's guilty of more negligence and stupidity than I'm prepared to tolerate," I said. "Whatever else happens, I'm going to demand his resignation. MTRI has suffered more than enough from his incompetence."

I'd expected her to be pleased, given all the trouble Carlson had caused her. But she surprised me. "I guess that's appropriate. It's sad, though. I know he's lost it, but he used to be a good scientist."

"That may be true, but what he's done now has resulted in at least one death, even if he didn't know that would be the consequence of his actions. And after what he's tried to do to you, I wouldn't waste your sympathy on him. He doesn't deserve it."

"I know. But it's still sad."

I shook my head. "Sorry, I can't share your generosity. Anyway, I want to ask you about something else. Leslie Farnsworth said that when she was reviewing your records, she noticed that the patients on aloxinor had a lower response rate than expected. Do you recall anything like that?"

Carolyn looked down for a moment, as if she was embarrassed. "I do. I don't know why, but only about half the aloxinor patients seemed to respond to the treatment. Which is fewer responders than there should have been."

"Did you ask Mark Heller about it?"

"No, I figured maybe it was just a sampling fluke. And to be honest, I didn't want to talk to Mark about it. I was afraid that if I said anything, his supporters at MTRI would say that I was just trying to sabotage his tenure case."

We were interrupted by an overweight, red-faced man, fully dressed in a black suit, tie, and long-sleeved white shirt. He was perspiring heavily, not unexpected since we were in the middle of a heat wave, with the temperature pushing ninety. "I'm AUSA Paul Markham. Is one of you Special Agent Richmond?"

Karen rose and extended her hand. "That's me. This is Dr. Carolyn Gelman, and this is Dr. Brad Parker."

Markham nodded absently. "Shall we proceed? Where's the prisoner?"

"He's in a room under guard," Karen said. "We can go back whenever you're ready. I wanted to update you a bit first, though. The hospital had a blood sample left from the first patient, Emily Weston. I had it tested. No surprise, it had a high level of thallium."

"Good," Markham said. "That directly links the suspect to Weston's murder."

"Indeed. And I also had his apartment searched this morning. It had been pretty well cleaned up, but they found white powder residue in a dresser drawer. Which tested out as thallium."

"So, we've got the asshole nailed. Why am I even here? It sounds like you have plenty to fry the prick. Why offer him anything?"

"Yes, but there's more going on than meets the eye," Karen said. "Orlov's just a hired gun. It's worth a deal if he can give us the man in charge."

"If you say so. All right, let's go."

Karen led off, and I followed Markham after her. He stopped and turned to me. "Excuse me, we're not having a party. Agent Richmond will suffice."

"No," Karen said. "I want him in on this. He knows who's who at the institute. Which means he's the only one who can tell if what Orlov says makes sense."

Markham shrugged ungraciously. "All right, come along. Let's get this over with."

Two state troopers were posted outside Orlov's room, where he was securely manacled to the bed. His head and chest were covered with bandages and an IV was attached to his arm. When he saw us enter, he looked at Karen and pressed a button attached to the IV. "Painkillers for what you did to me, FBI lady. All the fucking dope I want."

"Good for you," Karen sneered. "This is assistant US attorney Markham. He can make you an offer. In exchange for information."

Orlov looked Markham up and down. "I want witness protection. You are big enough to do that for me?"

"If you give us what we need," Markham said. "And if what you tell us holds up. Who hired you?"

"Yuri Derkach gave me the job."

Karen gave him a skeptical look. "The head of the Russian Mafia? Derkach hired you to come to Maine for this?"

Orlov rolled his eyes. "No, you know better than that. Derkach suggested that I take a call from a friend of his about it. So of course, I did. If Derkach suggests, it is like an order."

"Then who's the friend? Is he the one running the operation?" Karen asked.

"Yes. He offered very good money for me to come here with the job of messing up Carolyn Gelman's work."

"Are you talking about Carlson?"

Orlov gave a derisive snort. "No, I told you before. Carlson is just a dupe. The new boss said Carlson would accept me as a visiting scientist in his lab, that he sponsors many visitors. The boss sent me all the information to make an application, and it was just like he said. Carlson offered me a job, got visa for me, and here I am."

"Then who told you what to do? Did Carlson give you operational directions?"

"No, the boss would call me with his orders. At first, it was just to sabotage Gelman's research. That didn't work, but the boss thought that she wasn't going to get tenure anyway and it wouldn't matter."

He paused and looked over at me. "But then you came as director, and that changed things. The boss said you were supporting her. It meant I had to do more. I poisoned the first patient, and that still wasn't enough, so then I did the second."

"How did your boss know I was supporting Carolyn? Did Carlson tell him?"

Orlov shrugged. "Maybe. Carlson was one of his sources about what was going on at the institute. The boss said once that Carlson loved to gossip. Plus, the boss hacked your email. First the former director, now you."

"So that's how you knew that I took the pills to the pharmacy for analysis?"

Orlov nodded. "He told me to switch the poison ones back to the real thing, but I saw some were missing from the bottle. That's when I knew I had to get rid of the two of you."

"Was there anything else you were instructed to do?" Karen asked.

"Just a couple of side jobs. Hits on some drug dealers, one in New York, one in Boston. They had gone rogue, and the boss wanted them eliminated."

"Was your Boston job at the Harbor Inn in Revere?" Karen said.

"How you know that?"

"I figured there was a Russian mob connection, and we have you on the motel video. Your face doesn't show, but the body type fits. We're just waiting for ballistics to confirm the bullets came from your gun."

Orlov gave her what looked like an approving smile. "Very good. Now I've saved you the trouble."

Karen ignored his odd expression. "So now we have you for four murders. And you're not telling us anything we haven't figured out already. Giving us Derkach isn't worth shit. He's already well known to us, but we can't touch him in Moscow."

AUSA Markham stepped back in. "The fact is that everything you've said so far is useless, except for digging yourself into a deeper hole. There's no deal here; this is crap. A waste of my time."

"If you want something, you need to give us the name of your boss here. The one who actually directed the operation," Karen said.

"I don't know his name. I only get phone calls. They are always through a voice changer, so I don't even know what he sounds like."

Whoever's behind this is careful, I thought. Definitely not Carlson.

"How does he contact you?" Karen asked.

"I was given a phone that he uses to give me instructions. Money is just sent to one of my accounts in the Cayman Islands. I can give you the account information; maybe you can trace the deposits."

"We'll try, but I doubt it," Karen said. "Money transfers are easy to hide with dummy corporations. What if there's an emergency? You must have a way to contact him."

"There's a number I can call. I leave a coded message and he calls me back."

"Using the phone you were given?"

Orlov nodded.

"Very well, we need the phone," Karen said. "And the message you leave to make contact."

"And what do I get for that?" Orlov asked.

Markham answered. "If the phone takes us to the organizer of this shit storm, you'll get your witness protection."

"I had the phone with me last night, so you already have it," Orlov said. "You call the number in contacts and leave the message, 'Sorry, lost dog.' You will get a call back."

38

It was almost four by the time Karen finished doing paperwork with Markham and established that Orlov's phone was in the possession of the Maine state troopers. They had it at Troop A headquarters in Alfred, which turned out to be just north of Sanford, about forty-five minutes away. I was exhausted from the lack of sleep last night and suggested picking it up the next morning. But Karen insisted that she couldn't rest until she had her hands on the phone, so off we went.

Happily, the troopers were efficient and had the phone waiting for us. By five o'clock, we were back in the car heading home to Drakes Island. The phone was clutched tightly in Karen's hand.

I was fighting to stay awake and figured we might as well pick up something for dinner on the way home. But when I asked Karen what sounded good, my question was met by silence. When I looked over at her, I discovered that was because she'd fallen asleep, eyes closed and still holding the phone. It was somewhat reassuring that I wasn't the only one feeling the effects of what had been essentially a sleepless night.

Karen woke up when we pulled into the driveway and sleepily made her way upstairs, muttering something about needing a nap before dinner. It was past Rosie's dinner time, so I fed her and let her out in the yard. Then she followed me upstairs and we joined Karen in a nap.

It was dark when I woke up, with Karen and Rosie both asleep beside me. I figured that I'd slept for maybe two or three hours, but got a surprise when I looked at the bedside clock. Four o'clock, which had to mean that Tuesday night had become Wednesday morning and our naps had lasted something like nine hours. I guess we'd needed to make up the lost sleep.

Karen stirred when I sat up. "What time is it? Did you have dinner already?"

I smiled and stroked her hair. "Afraid we missed last night's dinner, Sleeping Beauty. It's four in the morning."

She stretched, finally waking Rosie as well. "No wonder my stomach's growling. What do we have for breakfast?"

I got up, promising to check out the breakfast possibilities. Rosie followed, her attention focused on food by the mention of breakfast. I'd started coffee, fed Rosie, and was working on scrambled eggs and bacon when Karen came down.

"Good morning, glad you could make it."

"It is a good morning." She held up Orlov's phone in her right hand. "Now that we have this."

I put breakfast on plates and took them out to the small glass table on our deck. Karen poured two mugs of coffee and followed.

"So, what's your plan for the phone?" I asked. "Call Orlov's boss and arrange a meeting?"

She shook her head. "Two problems. First, he'll know it isn't Orlov on the other end of the line. Although we could get around that by having Orlov make the call."

"Right, I thought of that. And the second?"

"Why would he agree to a meeting? He's stayed well hidden until now, and I don't think he's going to come out from behind his bush just because Orlov wants to chat."

"You could trace the call, no?"

She looked impatient. "We already have the number. It's a burner, of course. We could probably get a location for him, but it's the same phone as was used to send the blackmail photos, and we already know those calls came from Boston. I don't think any additional location info would be worth tipping our hand to get."

"Then what? You must be able to use it somehow."

"Yes, somehow. I'm just not sure how. Yet. But we do have some additional advantages."

"Which are?"

She ticked them off on her fingers. "First, he doesn't know that Orlov tried to burn us up and failed. Orlov says he told him that something needed to be done about us, but no specifics. Second, he doesn't know that we have Orlov or that we know about the thallium. And most important, we know how he gets his information about MTRI."

I nodded. "Courtesy of Carlson and my email. You're thinking we can use that against him?"

"Yep. Carlson's locked up tight; he hasn't told his boss the news. And you haven't put anything in email about the thallium pills or Carolyn being in the clear, right?"

"No, Carolyn's the only one who knows about any of it."

"Good. And I emphasized again yesterday that she shouldn't tell anybody. She said that she hadn't even told her husband."

"Not told her husband? You're kidding!"

Karen let out a small sigh. "I know. She said she didn't talk to him about her work, he wasn't interested. Pretty amazing."

"Pretty sick is more like it," I said.

She nodded. "Anyway, whoever the boss is, he thinks that Orlov is still in play, that Carolyn's trial is suspended, and that she'll go down in the upcoming tenure vote. And we know how to feed him disinformation."

She smiled coldly. A smile that I recognized from past experience. It meant no good for her adversary. "Now we just need to keep him thinking everything is normal while we figure out what lies to tell him. And how to trap the bastard."

"What do you think his motivation is? Whoever's responsible for this, it seems way over the top just to block Carolyn from getting tenure. Why would anyone care enough about a tenure case to import a Russian hitman and murder trial participants?"

"I know, it seems nuts," she said. "I suspect we'll only know the *why* when we know the *who*."

"Maybe. But I think knowing why could help us get to him."

"Of course. But that doesn't give us an answer."

"I may have an idea. Or at least a hunch."

"Yes?"

"Not yet." I got up from the table. "I need to go pay a visit to the institute and take care of some of the routine stuff that's accumulated, especially if we want everything to look normal. Let me poke around a bit and see what I can dig up."

39

Anna virtually attacked me with a handful of papers as soon as I walked through the office door. "Thank goodness you're here. I'm afraid some things have piled up that really need your attention."

I accepted the papers with a raised eyebrow. "Like what?"

"You'll see—just look through these. And deal with the urgent ones."

I gave her a mock salute and went into my office. It happily took only twenty minutes or so to deal with the matters that Anna had deemed pressing. Most were standard forms that just needed my signature.

Then there were two requests for interim funding by faculty members who were having trouble with grant renewals. I looked at those more carefully, before finally giving my approval. In both cases, I authorized less than the amount requested, but enough for them to keep their research going long enough to submit revised applications that hopefully would be successful. I thought they had a good shot.

Finally, there was a two-day-old memo from Carlson asking for—no, demanding—an additional two hundred and fifty square feet of lab space for a new microscope facility. That one I tossed into the blue recycle bin under my desk. More lab space wasn't something Carlson would be needing anytime soon, if ever.

That done, I composed an email to all MTRI tenured faculty, reminding them that we had a meeting scheduled to consider the tenure cases of Mark Heller and Carolyn Gelman. We would discuss and vote on both cases Friday afternoon at two o'clock. I figured that a business-as-usual email would be good for Orlov's boss to read.

Desk cleared, I settled in for the more interesting task at hand. Checking the original medical records of Heller's aloxinor trial. I hoped they matched the data he had reported—a response rate of around eighty percent. But given the discrepancy with Carolyn's observations, I needed to verify Heller's claim.

The records were all in the institute's patient database. I groaned when I saw the enormity of the file. There had been nearly four hundred patients enrolled in the trial, half of whom had been treated with aloxinor and half—the control group—with the standard treatment. Meaning that I'd have to examine a couple of hundred records to verify the outcomes of those patients who had received aloxinor.

Well, I wouldn't finish until I started…

Luckily, once I began reviewing the charts, it wasn't as difficult as I'd feared. The first page of each patient's file summarized the outcome as either response or no response, with response meaning at least a fifty percent reduction in tumor mass for a month or more. Unfortunately, the responses were almost always followed by relapse when the cancer developed resistance to the drug—the problem that both Carolyn and Heller now hoped to deal with.

I made two columns on a sheet of paper: Response and No Response. Then I started scanning the files, making a mark under the appropriate column as a running count of Roman numerals.

It was relatively quick going to just scan the first pages of each file, so I got through the set of aloxinor-treated patients in a couple of hours. Then I added up the score.

Response, 173 patients.

No Response, 42 patients.

A quick calculation told me that was a response rate of approximately eighty-one percent. Just as Heller had reported.

I sat back, feeling puzzled. The data analysis was no surprise. Of course, the raw data matched the published results. But how to explain the difference between this and what Carolyn had observed?

Idly, I started flipping through the chart of one of the patients who had responded, looking at the detailed record of his doctor visits. Suddenly, I did a double take. The patient's tumor had shrunk after aloxinor treatment, but only by thirty-two percent. Not the fifty percent reduction that was required to qualify as a response to treatment. The classification of this patient as a response was in error.

I looked at a second patient's records. This patient's tumor had shrunk by over seventy percent and had remained there for almost two months. Fine, a legitimate response. The next patient I looked at was also a legitimate response, so I started to relax. Maybe the misclassification of the first patient had been a clerical error.

But then I looked at a fourth. This patient's tumor had shrunk by just over fifty percent. Okay, good enough. But then I saw that it had grown back after only two weeks, not the month required for it to be called a response.

Having two out of four patients misclassified as responders was a bit much to accept as accidental error. I kept going. It was slow work, but three hours later I'd made it through the detailed records of forty patients that had been placed in the responder category. Of those, only twenty-five were properly classified as responders.

I did a quick calculation. If that applied to the whole data set, it meant that only sixty-two percent of the so-called responders were legitimate. Which would reduce the number of responders from 173 to 107. That was just about half of the 215 patients who had received aloxinor. Meaning the real response rate was around fifty percent, as Carolyn had observed. Not the eighty percent that Heller had claimed.

I stared at those numbers in shock and disgust. I still needed to go through the rest of the patient records, but it was clear enough.

Heller had faked the data to get his drug approved.

Aloxinor wasn't without effect, but it was no better than the standard treatment. By pretending that it was, Heller had committed the cardinal sin of medical science. He was guilty of a fraud that put the lives of patients at risk for his own personal advancement.

I gripped the edge of my desk and took a deep breath. What I wanted to do was storm into his office and wring his scrawny neck. At least figuratively, by throwing him out of MTRI and bringing his career to the disgraceful end he deserved. Likely followed by prison time for this.

But I held back. If he'd done this, was he also Orlov's boss? His possible motive for sabotaging Carolyn's career, even poisoning her patients to fake toxicity, was now clear enough. He had to stop her from discovering that aloxinor didn't work as advertised. And if he was willing to endanger patients' lives by faking clinical data, I wouldn't put murder past him.

This was potentially much more than scientific misconduct, and I needed to bring Karen in on it before I acted precipitously. Besides, she could help me work through the rest of the files.

I called Karen to tell her I was on my way home. And that we had a lot to talk about.

* * *

Karen had made a trip to Fisherman's Catch and was waiting with clam rolls, a side order of onion rings, and a bottle of wine when I got home. No way she was going to miss dinner two nights in a row. It was almost seven, so we ate and had a glass of wine while I told her the news.

When I finished, she polished off the last of the onion rings and regarded me pensively.

"I'm impressed. You've done a good day's work. Would anyone else have checked the patient records like you did?"

"You mean like the IRB? They would have verified the number of patients that responded, but probably not have gone all the way back to checking the individual patient visits. I just stumbled into doing that by accident."

She shook her head. "Well, you're right—I think Heller will see the inside of a cell for this. But the question still is whether he's the one who directed Orlov."

"It looks pretty good to me that he is. Stopping Carolyn's study before she wound up discovering that aloxinor didn't work as advertised is certainly a strong enough motive."

"Agreed. I'm just not sure I picture him in that role. But you think we should go through the remainder of the files?"

I sighed. "Yes, I think we should. Just to be complete."

"All right, let's get to it then. We can talk more about Heller when we're done."

I made a pot of strong coffee and gave Karen access to the files on her laptop. Then we split them up and started going through the remaining 175 patients that had been classified as responders. Even with both of us working, it took several hours, and it was nearly two in the morning when we finished.

I added up the numbers. "Altogether, we have 112 patients who responded. Not the 173 that Heller claimed. And 112 is just over half of 215, putting the response rate at fifty-two percent. Similar to what Carolyn was seeing."

Karen nodded, then yawned. "Okay, so Heller's a fraud. But is he a killer? I'm not convinced."

"What's holding you back? This is the first time we've seen anyone with a motive that was strong enough to make sense."

"No argument with that. But I guess I'm having two problems. First, I'm not convinced that Heller's sophisticated enough to hire someone like Orlov. You remember Orlov said he was initially contacted by Yuri Derkach, the biggest player in the Russian mob? How would someone like Heller be able to get Derkach working for him?"

I stretched, trying to relieve the pain in my back from being hunched over the computer for hours without a break. "I don't know, but that doesn't seem sufficient to rule Heller out. Maybe he has Russian relatives, or an uncle who's in the mob and has overseas connections. You can't just assume he's a nerd scientist."

Karen smiled. "Fair enough. But there's another thing. Orlov told us that his boss had him do a couple of hits on drug dealers, in addition to his major job of taking down Carolyn. That doesn't sound like Heller, either."

I thought about that one. Reluctantly, I had to admit she had a point. "Okay, guess I have to agree. So you think Heller's fraud is just a coincidence?"

She gave me a tolerant smile. "A coincidence? You know how much I like coincidences. No, I'm sure you've uncovered the motive. I'm just not convinced that Heller's our man, at least not the major player. But I think I know how to find out."

"Yes? Don't stop there."

"Not yet. I need to sleep on it and work through the details." She got up and kissed the top of my head. "Let's get some rest and talk about it in the morning. Don't worry, I have a leading role in mind for you."

40

It had been another long night, and I slept late. The clock said nearly eight when I woke up, and Karen was nowhere in sight. I slipped on bathing trunks and a T-shirt and made my way downstairs to the kitchen. I could just catch a glimpse of Karen and Rosie sitting on the beach. At least I assumed it was Karen underneath the enormous straw hat that pretty much obscured her face.

Coffee was ready and a box of scones was sitting on the kitchen counter, so I filled a mug, grabbed a scone, and headed down to the water. Rosie ran up to me in greeting, and I sat down on the blanket next to Karen.

"Morning, you're up early." I held up the scone. "Even made a trip to the bakery already."

"Glad you're awake, lazy bones. Afraid my mind was running too fast to sleep in with you. And I had to call the Bureau to do a little quick prep work."

I took a bite of the scone, dropping some crumbs that Rosie pounced on. "Mm, this is good. Blueberry?"

"I got some blueberry and some peach. Both good. Are you ready to hear the plan, or do you need to have your coffee first?"

"Go ahead, I can listen and eat at the same time."

"I want you to start by sending Heller an email asking him to meet with you. Make it a nice email for Orlov's boss to read, just in case it isn't Heller after all. Then, when Heller's in your office, I'll have Orlov call the contact number. If Heller takes the call, he's our man."

Maybe I needed the coffee after all, but I didn't see how this was going to work. "He's not going to take the call while he's with me. He may not even have the phone with him."

She rolled her eyes. "You think I'm stupid just because I have this ridiculous hat on? Of course he's not going to answer while you're there. Although he probably does carry the phone, since Orlov said he immediately returns calls to the contact number."

"So you figure I'll hear it ring?"

"Maybe, but more likely he keeps it in silent mode. That's what I had to call the Bureau about this morning. While he's in your office, we'll bug his, so we'll hear if he returns the call from there after your meeting. And I'll have watchers posted to keep an eye on him when he leaves, so we'll see if he goes somewhere else."

I smiled approvingly. "Got it. Good to know your head's still working underneath that monstrosity. What are you going to have Orlov say when he gets a return call? Just in case it's not Heller."

"Just that his first try at taking us out didn't work, but he'll take care of us in the next couple of days."

* * *

The email I sent Heller almost made me gag. A career in the upper reaches of academic administration had forced me to be less than honest all too often—but this was perhaps the worst.

Dear Mark -

Could we meet at eleven this morning for a half hour or so? As you probably know, the faculty meeting to consider your tenure case is

scheduled for Friday afternoon. Your record is of course overwhelmingly positive, and you can rest assured that I don't expect any problems. I'd just like to spend half an hour or so with you to make sure that I have everything straight. All my ducks in a row, as they say.
Brad

Heller arrived promptly, and I sent Karen a quick text to let her know he was here. She was at York Hospital with Orlov, and this would be her signal to have him make the call.

I waited expectantly for his phone to ring as I waved Heller over to my conference table. But no such instant gratification. As Karen had said, he probably had the phone on vibrate and would wait until after we finished to return the call. Meaning that I'd have to go through with this ridiculous charade of a meeting.

He put his laptop on the table as he sat down. "Thanks for meeting with me. I appreciate the opportunity to fill in any gaps you need to present my case. How can I help you?"

I needed to keep him here for half an hour to give Karen's agents time to bug his office and get into position to tail him when he left. But the last thing I felt like doing was having a bullshit conversation with him for that long. Fortunately, the laptop he'd brought with him suggested a way out.

"I don't have any specific questions. As I said, your record is quite clear and convincing." I was afraid he'd notice that I almost puked at that. But it seemed to go right by him, so I continued. "I think what I'd like is just a refresher overview of your recent work. And I see you brought your laptop, so maybe you could just give me a quick rerun of your tenure seminar. I don't need you to repeat the whole thing, but maybe just thirty minutes or so of the high points."

He smiled happily and dove right in. I was able to tune out and let him tell me again how wonderful he was. All I had to do was smile, nod, and make occasional encouraging noises until he ran out of steam forty minutes later.

I stood up and offered my hand. "Perfect, that was just what I needed. I'm sure there won't be any problems tomorrow, but now everything's fresh in my mind, just in case any questions come up. And don't worry, I'll be in touch to let you know the results of the vote as soon as the meeting's over."

I resisted the urge to go wash my hands when he left. Instead, I texted Karen again.

He just left my office. No ringing phone. Let me know what he does now.

I sat back to wait. It would take a few minutes for Heller to get back to his office and return the call.

But Karen's text came in immediately.

Orlov's boss returned his call fifteen minutes ago. It's not Heller.

41

Orlov lay manacled to the hospital bed, plotting and fuming. The lawyer—AUSA Markham—had turned out to be a prick. A man of no honor, like prosecutors everywhere. To have the balls to storm in here and say the deal's off because their trick didn't work out. I could have told them Heller wasn't the boss. He's just another jerk scientist, not someone with the money and connections to know Derkach.

It was time to get out, escape from this small-town confinement. Before the bastard Markham made good on his threat of life imprisonment.

The two state troopers guarding him were both stationed in the room. At all times, except when they wanted to eat and one of them went to the cafeteria to get food. Which would be soon. Their shift had started at three, and it was now approaching six o'clock.

As if on cue, the smaller of the two looked at his watch. "I'm hungry. We've been at this for three hours. Want something to eat?"

"Sure, bring me some of whatever delicacy the cafeteria's serving up tonight. I'll stay here with our boy."

"You'll be okay alone with him?"

The second trooper laughed. He was a big man, six-two and solid muscle. "A little pipsqueak like that? Take your time, I'll be fine."

Orlov waited a few minutes after the first trooper left. Then he moaned and curled up in the bed. "Help me, I've got to get to the bathroom."

"Oh, for Christ's sake. Here, I'll get your bedpan. You can piss in that."

"No, my stomach's cramping. I'm going to shit all over. Quick, I can't hold it much longer!"

"All right, all right. Hold on."

The trooper came over and, with his gun in one hand, unlocked the handcuffs from the bedpost. Orlov didn't hesitate. He ignored the gun and chopped the trooper viciously across his throat. Orlov watched him crumble to the floor, his windpipe crushed. Then he broke the trooper's neck to finish the job.

Using the trooper's key, Orlov finished removing the cuffs. Then he put on the trooper's clothes. They were too big by far, but he rolled up sleeves and pant legs so at least he wouldn't trip over himself on the way out. Awkward but it would have to do.

He was able to make his way to the front entrance before anyone noticed. Then the second trooper came out of the cafeteria and saw him. He yelled and went for his gun, but Orlov used the dead trooper's gun to shoot him first. Then he ran to the parking lot, where a woman was pulling up in a Mercedes sedan. He roughly shoved her to the ground and took the car.

They'd be after him, of course, but he wasn't worried. He'd pulled off escapes before, from much tougher and better policed places than southern Maine. His safe house—an isolated cabin about a hundred miles north—was waiting. He'd set it up when he first arrived in Maine, taking advantage of the state's large amount of sparsely populated forest area. Everything he needed was there. Money, clothes, a new passport, and weapons. He'd trade cars soon and use the back roads. Once there, he'd fix himself up with a wig, a beard and mustache, and colored contacts to change his brown eyes to blue.

When he was ready, it would be an easy run north to the Canadian border. And from there to the Cayman Islands to pick up his money.

But there was something he had to do first. A debt that had to be paid.

42

The waiter brought our second round of margaritas as Karen and I finished off an appetizer of steamed clams. We had a window table at Hobbs Harborside with a stunning view of Wells Harbor. It was one of our favorite places, and Karen had suggested we come here to enjoy the evening rather than brooding over our failure to trap Heller. It was only partially working—but then we were still waiting for our baked stuffed lobsters.

I took a sip of my fresh margarita and asked the question that was foremost in both our minds. "If it's not Heller, then who? I can't believe everything's not based on trying to cover up Heller's fraud."

"No argument with that. And we don't know that Heller's innocent. Just that he's not the one giving Orlov orders."

"You think he knows about Orlov? And who's responsible for directing him?"

She sipped her drink. "Maybe, maybe not. I'm debating whether to have him picked up for some tough questioning."

The waiter interrupted to clear the now-empty bowl of steamers, and our lobsters were served with a flourish. When he finished, I asked, "Why debate? At least we'd find out how much he knows."

Being Karen, she took a big bite of her lobster before answering. Then she looked up with a grin. "Mm, I like this place. But Heller. The downside of bringing him in is that it might send a warning to whoever we're after. Plus, I'm not sure how much we'd get out of him. If he is implicated, he's probably smart enough to keep his mouth shut."

I tried the lobster, too. It really was good. "Yes, Heller's probably smart enough to ask for a lawyer and keep quiet. But if not squeezing him, what's the next move?"

She answered with a question. "Who else would want to protect the status of aloxinor? It's important to Heller for his career, but how much money is involved?"

"A successful lung cancer drug? Probably hundreds of millions. Maybe more."

She raised an eyebrow. "Wow. I knew we'd be talking big bucks, but that's quite a sum. Certainly enough to be a motive for murder. Who gets the payoff?"

"Most of it goes to the pharmaceutical company that backed the development of the drug and holds the patent. Pharmathor. I'm not sure of the details of the aloxinor deal, but typically five percent or so would come back to MTRI. Maybe half of that would then go to Heller, either personally or for research support."

"So if we follow the money, which works more often than not, we should be thinking about Pharmathor. And a pharmaceutical company is interesting for a couple of other reasons. For one thing, they'd be likely to have thallium, which is otherwise hard to get. That's where the woman who poisoned her husband in the New Jersey case got it."

"I remember you mentioning that," I said. "Plus, I bet you're thinking that a pharmaceutical company might also be involved with trafficking pain killers, right?"

She rewarded me with a smile. "You're reading my mind."

"Hang on, let me see what Pharmathor makes."

I took out my phone and Googled Pharmathor. Then I went to the products section of their website. "Looks like mostly cancer drugs. A few antivirals. But I don't see any pain meds."

She finished off the last bite of her lobster before answering. "Still, someone in the industry could easily enough have pain killer connections. Where are they located?"

I checked the website. "In Cambridge. I think the street address is in the Kendall Square area."

"Interesting. That's where the blackmail photos were sent from, remember?"

I nodded. "I do. You think we're on to something?"

"Maybe. I think we should figure out who at Pharmathor was involved in aloxinor development. Presumably they'd be in line to profit from its success."

Before I could answer, her phone rang. She looked annoyed. "Hang on a minute, I better see what this is."

She answered with a curt, "Agent Richmond." Then her face fell and she was quiet for what seemed like a long time. Finally, she spoke again. "All right. We're at Hobbs Harborside. We'll wait for them here."

She turned to me with a shake of her head. "Orlov escaped. He killed both state troopers who were guarding him and stole a car at the hospital. He's in the wind."

"Jesus Christ! How'd he manage that?"

"I don't know. I guess there's a reason he's considered one of the best." She reached across the table and took my hand. "I'm afraid they think he's coming after us. Especially me, since I'm the one who took him down. They're sending two units to keep watch over us."

43

The woman that answered spoke in Russian. "Da?" She sounded abrupt, annoyed by the call.

"I need to speak to him," Orlov said. Also in Russian.

"He doesn't take random calls."

"You know who this is?"

"Of course."

"Then put him on the fucking phone!"

"Wait, I'll ask."

Several moments passed. Orlov almost ended the call. If he had to, he'd go back to Russia and do this in person.

Finally, another voice came on. Orlov recognized it immediately. Derkach.

"What do you want? It better be important for you to call this number."

"I need the name of the man you set me up with."

Derkach made a harsh, guttural noise. "You know I can't give you that."

"He's broken our bargain. I need to make him pay."

"Explain."

"I've been arrested. I escaped and I'm in a safe place now. But it was his fault this happened. He insulted me and forced me to do something stupid against my judgment. I protested, but he wouldn't listen. And now catastrophe, all because he broke the code."

"Can you get out of the country?"

"Of course. But not until I deal with him."

"You realize we'll be finished if I give you the name of a client? I won't be able to use you again."

"I understand. I have funds for a comfortable retirement waiting for me in the islands."

Derkach gave him the name.

44

Trying to sleep with Karen's gun in bed between us hadn't made for a restful night. Nonetheless, we'd been undisturbed, and the two cops who'd stayed and spent the night outside in their car reported that there'd been no sign of Orlov.

"I don't think he's after me, anyway," Karen said the next morning.

I took another big gulp of coffee, hoping to clear the cobwebs. "Why not? You're the one who took him down. And hurt him in the process."

"Yes, but I'm a professional. He'll view my arresting him as just business, part of the game. But his boss is another story. You saw how willing Orlov was to give him up to us. He feels that his boss betrayed him, which makes him responsible for the mess Orlov's in now."

"Meaning you think Orlov's planning to take revenge on his boss?"

"That'd be my guess," Karen said. "Unless he's just going to head for Canada. In either case, I don't think he's going to make another run at us."

I gave an exaggerated sigh of relief. "Glad you think so. But how can he be going after his boss if he doesn't know who he is?"

"I wouldn't be surprised if he knows more than he's been willing to tell us." She shrugged. "But that's not going to help us any. Let's get back to figuring out who at Pharmathor made a profit from aloxinor. And stands to take a fall if Heller's fraud is discovered."

"All right. I can dig up the aloxinor contract and see who signed for Pharmathor."

"Maybe later," she said. "But there's no reason to assume the official signatory is the organizer, is there?"

"No, I suppose not. What then?"

"Let's go talk to Carlson. I suspect that he'll be cooperative after having spent the last couple of nights in a cell."

* * *

The Wells City Jail was a small holding facility in the police station, meant for temporary housing of local prisoners. Most arrests in Wells were for property crimes, so a prisoner being held on a murder conspiracy charge was something of a local celebrity. Two cops brought him in handcuffs to the small interrogation room where Karen and I were waiting. They pushed him into a chair across the bare wooden table from us and stood in the back of the room.

"You can take the cuffs off and leave us alone," Karen said.

"I don't think that's wise, ma'am," one of the cops replied. "He's a dangerous felon."

Karen rolled her eyes and showed her badge. "Don't worry, I can handle him."

Carlson rubbed his wrists when they took the cuffs off. The three nights he'd been locked up clearly hadn't agreed with him. His skin was gray, his eyes were puffy, and he smelled like rancid cheese—no doubt from wearing the same clothes he'd had on when Karen arrested him.

"Please, can you get me out of here?" he pleaded. "You know I'm not involved in any crazy murder scheme."

"That depends," Karen said. "We need some information."

"Anything. I'll tell you whatever you want to know."

"Are you aware that Heller's data on aloxinor was faked?" I asked.

Carlson's eyes looked like they were about to pop out of his head. "What? That's impossible!"

"I went back over the primary data from his trial. He fudged the patient records to get a response rate of eighty percent. The real response rate was only fifty percent, which wouldn't have been good enough to get FDA approval."

Some of Carlson's usual cockiness returned. "He couldn't have. I reviewed those data myself for the IRB. I remember going through the patient records and counting up the number of responses. My count matched his exactly."

"You looked at the chart summary for each patient?"

He nodded emphatically. "Absolutely. And the number was right."

I tried to look as disgusted as I felt. "Too bad you didn't do your job right and go through the full record of patient visits. I did. And the visit reports don't match the summaries. That's what Heller faked."

"Oh my God." He put his head in his hands. "Oh my God, how could he?"

He looked up trembling. "What's going to happen? I didn't know, you have to believe me."

I actually did. He was again guilty of incompetence and negligence, but I didn't think he was part of the fraud. I looked at Karen and she nodded. Then she took over.

"Heller will be disgraced and thrown out of his profession," she said. "And in all likelihood go to prison. What will happen to you is going to depend on what you have to tell us next, so think carefully about what you have to say."

"I'll tell you anything. Did Heller hire that man? Turgenev, or whatever you said his name is."

"Orlov," Karen said. "No, Heller's not his boss."

Carlson's eyes widened in panic. "It's not me! Please, you have to believe me."

"We know that," Karen said. "And you're going to help us figure out who it was."

"How? I told you, I don't know anything about this."

I jumped in. "You have connections at Pharmathor, going back even before Heller came to MTRI, right?"

"Yes, Pharmathor has supported my research for some time. I first introduced them to Mark."

"Who at Pharmathor was involved with development of aloxinor?"

"There have been several people. The project officer for both Mark's project and my own lab is now Sharon Talbot, one of their Research and Development people."

"Did she initially sponsor the project?"

"No, that was Arthur Friedland. But he got a promotion and left the project soon after aloxinor won approval. Now I believe he's one of their vice presidents, or something big like that."

"All right," Karen said. "Let's see where that takes us."

She got up and knocked on the door.

"Wait. Please. Can I get out of here now?" Carlson whined.

"Not yet. If your information helps, then maybe."

"As long as you agree to resign from MTRI immediately," I added.

We watched as the guards took him away. Then I said, "I remember Arthur Friedland's name. Claire Houghton mentioned him. He's a member of the BTI board of directors. The one who pushed her to fire me as director."

"Sounds like we should give Mr. Friedland a closer look," Karen said.

"Let's see if I can find out more about him." I used my phone to go to the Pharmathor website. The senior management team was listed with their pictures, including Arthur Friedland. I clicked on Friedland's name, which brought up a pop-up bio.

"Interesting. He came to Pharmathor over ten years ago in their Research and Development division. Then, like Carlson said, he was promoted to a top post around the time that aloxinor became a success story. And guess where he was before Pharmathor."

Karen looked impatient. "Okay, I'll bite."

"Purdue Pharmaceuticals. The manufacturers of OxyContin. He left just before the scandal about their marketing practices broke."

"The overly aggressive marketing that people think contributed to the opioid crisis? And that led to criminal convictions of three of their executives?"

"The same."

She pursed her lips and nodded. "Let's go pay Mr. Friedland a visit."

45

We stopped at the Drakes Island house for some prep work. Karen said she wanted to get a backup team to cover us at Pharmathor headquarters and went upstairs to call her Boston office. I went out on the deck with my iPad and sent an email to MTRI faculty saying that a personal emergency had come up and I wouldn't be in today. The meeting to discuss tenure cases would have to be rescheduled for early next week. Theoretically, my directorship would be over after today, but I didn't think there'd be a problem extending it once I brought Claire Houghton up to date on recent events.

Rosie jumped up on my lap and we watched the sandpipers dart in and out of the surf while I waited for Karen. I wasn't sure what she had planned for our visit to Pharmathor, but I was looking forward to it with nervous anticipation. With any luck, confronting Friedland would bring us to a conclusion. As long as Orlov wasn't after her for revenge. Maybe it would be a good idea for me to start carrying a weapon until he was out of the picture.

My thoughts of protecting Karen were interrupted by my phone's ringtone. I didn't recognize the number, but I took the call anyway. Maybe someone from MTRI was calling in response to my email.

A deep voice spoke with what I'd come to recognize as a Russian accent. "You're a dead man, Parker. You and your bitch FBI girlfriend." Then the caller disconnected.

I broke into a sweat. Orlov! I jumped up and ran into the house, to find Karen coming down the stairs.

"Orlov just called me! He's coming for us."

She looked at me with a mischievous smile and held up a phone. "Good, you thought it was Orlov. You can relax, it was just me. With the new voice changer software."

"What?"

She laughed. "I sent our tech guys a tape of Orlov and had them install software on his phone to deepen my voice and give it a Russian accent, at least somewhat like his. From your reaction, I guess it worked."

I didn't know whether to be angry or just shocked. "What the hell for? You almost gave me a heart attack."

"Sorry about that. I needed to give it a test run. C'mon, I'll explain while we drive to Boston."

* * *

Karen kept a heavy foot on the gas, so we were turning onto Storrow Drive in Boston in just over an hour. Just enough time for her to brief me on her plan and for me to get my head around the act I was supposed to pull off. It'd be tricky, but unlike some of her ploys in the past, it didn't seem dangerous. I was good to go by the time she turned off Storrow Drive to cross the Longfellow Bridge into the Kendall Square area of Cambridge.

Largely because of its proximity to MIT, Kendall Square had become a world hub of biotechnology. It was home to more than a hundred biotech and pharmaceutical companies, including some of the giants of the industry, such as Genzyme, Biogen, Alnylam, and Bristol Myers Squibb. It felt like we were driving through a canyon surrounded by towering steel-and-glass buildings as we made our way to Pharmathor headquarters on Third Street and parked in front of the building. Illegally, of course.

A security guard inside the entrance pointed us to an elevator bank and told us that Mr. Friedland's office was on the twenty-second floor, along with the other top executives. We exited the elevator in a large waiting area and were greeted by a young dark-haired woman at a glass-top reception desk. Karen took a seat in one of the leather lounge chairs near the elevator, while I told the receptionist that I was here to see Arthur Friedland.

"Do you have an appointment?" she asked.

"No. I'm Professor Brad Parker, director of MTRI. An emergency has come up that I need to discuss with Mr. Friedland immediately."

"I'm sorry, Mr. Friedland's fully booked today. I'm afraid he's a very busy man, but if you could call his office to make an appointment, I'm sure his administrator will be able to set something up for you."

I shook my head. "He'll want to see me now. Just let him know who I am and that I've uncovered a problem with Mark Heller's research. I can assure you, it's something that he'll want to know about without delay."

She frowned but said to wait a moment and went down the hall to relay the message. I resisted the temptation to follow her and barge into Friedland's office. If the message I'd planted didn't get me a meeting, then he wasn't our man.

But she returned in a few minutes with a smile pasted on her face. "This must be your lucky day. He's had a cancellation and says he'd be happy to meet with you."

She led me to an office in the northeast corner, where an administrative assistant greeted me, knocked on the mahogany door behind her desk, and ushered me into a cavernous office with oil paintings hanging on mahogany-paneled walls, an oversize oriental rug, and luxury antique furnishings. Friedland rose from behind a black executive desk with carved leather panels to greet me with a vague smile. He looked to be in his mid-forties, with a full head of bright red hair and a tan that looked like he spent considerable time in the sun.

"Professor Parker. I'm pleased to finally meet you. Thank you for coming to see me." He indicated an overstuffed guest chair across from the desk. "I'm afraid it's a busy day, though. What can I do for you?"

"I'm afraid I have some bad news. But I'm glad you could see me because I wanted to tell you immediately, before it became known by anyone else."

I paused to let that sink in. His expression darkened and he prodded impatiently. "What's the problem? You've got my attention, now speak."

"Yes, I'm sorry. It's Mark Heller's research. You may know he's coming up for tenure, and I was reviewing his records."

I could see the tension rising in him. "And? Spit it out, I don't have all day."

"He faked the data from his clinical trial of aloxinor. He claimed a patient response rate of eighty percent, which got the drug approved. But when I reviewed the original records, the response rate was only around fifty percent. Not good enough to have won FDA approval."

His eyes widened and he sat bolt upright. "Holy shit! That's terrible! Are you sure?"

"I'm afraid so. Here, I brought examples of some of the records. You can see for yourself."

I showed him two of the files where Heller had falsely claimed that patients had responded. His attention was riveted as he skimmed through several others that I'd brought along. It gave me a good opportunity to slip the bug Karen had given me down the side of my chair cushion.

He had himself under control when he finished. "It's unbelievable that anyone could do this. We'll have to get this drug off the market immediately. What a terrible thing. Have you notified the FDA?"

"I haven't told anyone yet. I wanted to let you know first. I know this is a big blow to Pharmathor, and I wanted to give you the opportunity to deal with it before it became a public scandal."

"Thank you. Very much indeed. I truly appreciate that. Now I'd better get on the phone to the FDA and get a recall started. You've done a great service to everyone by exposing this."

I stood up. "I'm glad to help. I know that you've been a good friend to MTRI. I'll head back now and confront Heller when I get there. Will that give you enough time to get ahead of the situation?"

"Yes, I'll call the FDA right away. Thank you again."

He'd already picked up a phone by the time I left the office.

46

His table on the café patio was right across the street from the entrance to Pharmathor, with a clear view of everyone going in or out. He ordered a cheeseburger and iced tea and sat back to wait for the boss to leave the building for lunch. A word with him on the street so the bastard would know what was coming. Then a clean shot to the head. His car was parked a block away, so a quick escape and a change of disguise would be easy.

Then the red Volvo parked in front of Pharmathor, and Parker and the FBI woman got out. What the hell! Had they somehow figured out who the boss was? Could she be that smart?

He watched them go into the building. They must know. He felt real admiration. What a woman she was. Perhaps the strongest adversary he'd faced.

He waited a few minutes, threw some money on the table, and followed them in. He didn't like the unexpected to interfere with his plans, but this was too intriguing to ignore.

They got into an elevator and he watched as it ascended to the top floor. Where Friedland's office was located.

He followed in the next elevator. When he got off, Parker was heading into one of the offices and the woman was sitting in the waiting area. She glanced at him briefly, but showed no sign of recognition. No surprise there; he was confident of his disguise.

He took a chair near her. He wasn't sure of his next move, but having her and Parker here with his target added an intriguing twist to the game. He wouldn't hurt the woman, of course. But Parker was just a nosy troublemaker. Taking care of him together with the boss would be an added bonus.

47

Karen's phone was ringing when I got back to the reception area. She motioned me to sit beside her and held the phone up so I could listen.

"Yes," she said.

The voice on the other end of the line had a mechanical, almost robotic, tone. "You sound odd. Everything all right?"

Karen made a face and crossed her fingers. "I'm fine, must just be the connection. I hear you okay."

"All right." Karen gave me a thumbs up. Her try at mimicking Orlov's voice had passed muster.

"You have to move quickly," the voice on the phone continued. "Parker knows about Heller faking the aloxinor results. He just left here, going back to MTRI. He'll tell people when he gets there, so you need to intercept and finish him first. Then get the damned woman, too."

"Not a problem," Karen said. "I'll stop him midway."

She ended the call and got up with a grin. "Got him."

I followed her back down the hall to Friedland's office, where she showed her badge to the administrative assistant and unceremoniously stormed through the door.

Friedland jumped up from behind his desk, his eyes widening in shock. "Parker! What the hell's going on?" Looking at Karen, he added, "Who's this?"

Karen held up her badge. "Special Agent Richmond, FBI. Arthur Friedland, you're under arrest. Turn around and put your hands behind your back."

"What the hell for? You're fucking crazy."

"The murder of Emily Weston and the attempted murder of Fred Reed, for starters." Karen held up the phone. "Do you recognize this? It's the number you just called. It used to belong to your hired killer, Alexei Orlov. Now it's mine." She started to play back the phone call.

Friedland forced a laugh. "I don't know who that voice is, but it's not me. Doesn't sound anything like me."

I reached under the side of the chair cushion I'd been sitting on, pulled out the recording device I'd planted, and hit play. "How about this? Sound more like you?"

Suddenly I heard a door close behind me. A short man with long gray hair and a bushy mustache stood there smiling at us. When he spoke, I recognized a Russian accent. It was as familiar as the gun in his hand, with a silencer attached to the barrel.

"I'm so pleased to find all of you waiting for me."

Friedland looked like he was in shock. "Who the hell are you?"

Karen spoke almost simultaneously. "Orlov?"

He gave a harsh guttural laugh. "Yes, it is me. Orlov. You like my disguise?"

Friedland started to come around from behind the desk. "Thank God you're here. You can get rid of these two."

Orlov smiled. "Don't worry, I'll take care of them. But first, you must pay."

"Of course, no problem." Friedland picked up a phone. "I'll transfer the money to your usual account."

"No. This time there is a different kind of debt to be paid. What you owe for violating our bargain and getting me caught. I told you at the beginning that I made the rules. But you broke our contract by insisting that I go against my judgment and give a whole bottle of poison pills to our last target. That led these two to me."

Friedland turned pale and was trembling uncontrollably by the time Orlov finished. "Anything," he managed to say. "I'll do whatever you want."

Orlov laughed again. "You don't need to do anything. You only have to die."

Then he shot Friedland twice in the face.

48

Orlov moved the gun to cover Karen and me as Friedland fell to the floor. We were helpless. I got ready to throw myself at him in a final act of desperation. There was no question that he'd shoot me before I reached him, but maybe I could give Karen an opening. At least the possibility of a chance to get out of this.

"Don't worry," he said. "I'm not going to kill the two of you. I have another use for you." He looked directly at Karen. "Besides, you're a professional. Like me, not traitor scum like this piece of shit." He nudged Friedland's body with his foot. "You caused me trouble, but by doing your job. And you are good. How did you figure him out?"

Karen somehow managed to remain calm. Or at least look like she was. "We knew it wasn't Heller, and Friedland also stood to make money from the aloxinor fraud. Plus, he had a background in manufacturing and distributing OxyContin, so that fit with your hit on the drug dealers in Boston."

Orlov nodded. "Smart lady. Yes, he had access to a large supply of drugs, he said from his previous job. That and aloxinor made him a very rich man." He spat on the corpse. "But a very stupid one."

He turned to me. "Use her handcuffs to secure her to the conference table. Then you'll come with me, just in case I need a hostage."

"Let him go," Karen said. "I'm more valuable to you. Nobody's going to take a chance on a senior agent getting killed."

Orlov smiled pleasantly. "No, I don't think so. I like you, but you know too many tricks. Your friend will be easier to manage." He waved the gun at her. "Give him your handcuffs and sit by the conference table. Hands behind you."

Karen started to protest, but I cut her off. At least she'd be safe this way. "Please, Karen. Do as he says, it'll be all right. He has no reason to hurt me."

I didn't think that was true. The fact was, he'd have no reason to let me go. But it was our best play for now.

She closed her eyes and took a deep breath. Then she turned to Orlov. "You'll let him go later?"

"Of course," he said. "Once I'm out of Boston."

I was pretty sure she didn't trust him, but there wasn't any other choice. She followed his directions and gave me her handcuffs. Then she sat and I secured her hands around the table leg.

Orlov tossed me a handkerchief. "Now use this to gag her."

I obliged. At least Karen would survive, although my eventual fate was less clear.

Orlov checked my work when I'd finished.

"Good enough," he pronounced. "Now come over here and stay by my side. We're going to walk through the reception area and get on the elevator together." He pressed the gun into my ribcage. "This gun will be at your back."

We stepped over the body of Friedland's administrative assistant in the outer office—another one of Orlov's collateral victims—and exited into the hallway leading to the reception area. Nobody paid any attention as we made our way to the elevator. Two people got off when it reached our floor, and Orlov shoved me into the empty car. "We'll take this down to the lobby and turn right when we leave the building. My car is a block away."

The gun stayed pressed into my back as we walked down the street, side by side like close friends. People were heading out for lunch and the street was busy, giving me what I figured would be my best chance for escape. If I could somehow distract him, maybe I could break free and duck away in the crowd. Once he had me alone in the car, shooting me would be all too easy.

Except Orlov was no fool. He kept a tight grip as we walked past oblivious passersby. Desperation mounted as I waited for an opportunity that didn't come. Maybe when we reached the car and he had to open the doors… In any case, I'd go for it then. It would be my last chance.

I steeled my nerves as Orlov said, "It's the blue sedan two cars down." We were almost at the point of no return.

Suddenly, there was a shout behind me. "Parker! Where's Richmond?"

Orlov's grip loosened as he turned to see who was behind us. I didn't know what was happening, but this was my moment.

I swiveled and kicked him hard in the knee. Then I dove to the side between a line of parked cars.

I heard the muffled noise of his silencer and felt a bullet whip past me.

I waited helplessly for the next shot. He wouldn't miss twice.

But instead I heard someone yell, "FBI, drop your weapon!"

Orlov started to turn. Then there were three loud booms and his chest exploded as he fell to the ground.

A man and a woman ran toward us. The man stopped to check Orlov, although the gaping wounds in his chest made it pretty obvious that he was dead.

The woman reached me as I was trying to sit up. "Are you all right?"

"Yes, I'm okay. Thank God you were here, whoever you are."

"Agents Kaufman and Morris. We're the backup that Agent Richmond requested. Where is she?"

"She's safe. In Arthur Friedland's office, the Pharmathor building. You'll find another body there with her." I glanced over at Orlov's remains. "The man who was his boss."

49

The large conference room we used for faculty meetings was packed by the time I arrived Tuesday morning for the long-anticipated vote on tenure candidates. I took my seat at the head of the table and counted noses. Everyone was there, so I rapped on the table to bring the meeting to order.

But before I could even get started, Ann Osborne—one of the faculty members who'd been strongly opposed to Carolyn—spoke up. "Excuse me, I don't see Tom Carlson. You need to wait for him."

I smiled to myself. The temptation was to tell her that it was time for the meeting to convene and I didn't need to wait for anybody. But her interruption gave me a good lead-in to the issues I needed to address, so I went with it.

"I'm afraid that Dr. Carlson won't be joining us. He's resigned his position at MTRI, effective last Friday. The last time I saw him, he was in the Wells jail, being held on conspiracy charges."

The room erupted. Some of the faculty just stared at me with open mouths, but most started babbling incoherently.

I waited several minutes for the noise to die down. When it finally did, Osborne held up one of the manila folders that Anna had distributed around the table. She looked somewhat chastened, but her usual aggression was still evident.

"What's with these information packets?" she asked. "Why is there only material on Gelman, not on Mark Heller?"

All eyes turned to me, and I delivered my second shock of the day. "Mark Heller is also no longer with us," I said. "I terminated his position based on the morals clause in our employment contract. He faked his clinical trial results with aloxinor and is currently under arrest for criminal fraud."

This time they all just stared at me in shock. Finally, Leslie Farnsworth raised her hand for recognition. "I think you'd better tell us what's been going on," she said.

I took them through it, just leaving out some of the more personal parts. Like the night I'd spent at Carolyn's place and the details of the night that Orlov had come after Karen and me. They were still staring silently, their expressions a mixture of shock and awe, when I finished.

"So the only case before us today is the promotion and tenure of Carolyn Gelman," I concluded. "I'd like to ask Leslie Farnsworth to summarize Gelman's dossier and report on the status of her ongoing clinical trial."

I'd brought Leslie into the picture over the weekend and told her that I'd call on her for this presentation. She briefly presented Carolyn's relevant background information and then went through her review of Carolyn's clinical trial in detail, emphasizing that there was no drug toxicity and pointing out that the results to date looked good. When she finished, I opened the floor for general discussion.

At this point, I didn't know what to expect. It was hard to imagine that there would still be opposition, but the hostility toward Carolyn had run deep. I suspected the argument was about to start when Ann Osborne raised her hand.

"I don't think further discussion is needed," she said. "I move for a vote in favor of Carolyn Gelman's tenure and promotion, with apologies to her from those of us who were taken in by Carlson and Heller."

The room erupted in applause and several loud calls of "Second."

I sighed with relief. "Thank you. We have a motion on the floor with several seconds. Is there any further discussion before we vote?"

I searched the room with my eyes. Silence.

"Very well," I said. "Please raise your hand to signify a vote in favor of tenure and promotion for Carolyn Gelman."

All hands went up. Carolyn's vindication was unanimous.

* * *

Karen was sitting in my chair when I got back to the office. "Everything go okay?" she asked.

I gave her a thumbs-up. "Yep, no problems. Ready to go congratulate Carolyn?"

Karen got up with a grin as I retrieved a bottle of champagne from my minifridge and grabbed the three glasses I'd brought in for the occasion.

Carolyn answered my knock on her office door with a look of trepidation. It changed to an expression of shock when I held out the champagne and said, "Congratulations, Professor Gelman!"

"Oh my God! They voted for me? I can't believe it!"

Karen laughed. "That's what he says. I guess we can trust him."

"Oh my God!" Carolyn repeated. Then she flung her arms around me. "Thank you! I didn't think you could ever get them to support me."

"It wasn't me," I said. "It was your record, your accomplishments. All they had to do was listen with open minds to what you've done."

I could see the news sinking in as a broad smile of relief spread across her face. She let me go with a final squeeze. "If it wasn't for you, I never would have had a chance. I can't thank you enough. I owe you everything."

Karen cleared her throat. "Okay, I'm thirsty. Let's pop this champagne."

Carolyn smiled. "Come on in."

We sat at her desk and I managed to get the bottle open without incident. Karen poured three glasses and I raised mine in a toast. "To MTRI's newest tenured professor."

We clinked glasses and sipped. "I think you'll find a very different attitude on the part of your colleagues now," I said. "It was just Heller and Carlson that poisoned the atmosphere against you. With them gone, you can look forward to some big changes in the way you're treated around here."

"You two are really something," Carolyn took another sip of champagne and grinned. "You not only fixed MTRI and got me tenure, but you even arranged a party for me."

"I'm sure it's nothing compared to what your husband will have in store for you later," Karen said. "Do you want to call and give him the good news?"

Carolyn's smile faded. "No, he doesn't like to be interrupted at work. Anyway, he won't be home for a few days. He's staying in Portland until the end of the week." She shrugged. "It'll just be me and the kids tonight."

I was about to ask if he'd known her tenure vote was today, but I realized that of course he did. He just didn't care. Lousy bastard.

That hadn't escaped Karen either. "I'm sorry," she said. "Do you want to have dinner with us? We can continue the celebration over lobsters."

Carolyn turned to her with a weak smile. "Thank you, but no. You've done enough already. More than enough."

Then she looked at Karen pointedly. "You think I should leave him, don't you?"

"I don't know," Karen said. "Marriages are complicated. Mine was a disaster."

I couldn't contain myself. Against my better judgment, I spoke up. "Damn right you should leave him. He doesn't deserve you. And he treats you like shit."

"I know," she murmured. "But the kids need a father."

"Not just any father. He's not really there for them, either, is he?"

"No, I guess not." She sighed. "I'll have to try and think about it. Maybe now that the professional stuff is sort of settled, I can deal with my personal problems. Anyway, you've been such a good friend. I'll miss you."

We stood, and Carolyn hugged me again. As we were leaving, Karen turned and gave her a hug, too. "Don't hesitate to call if you need us," she said. "Or if you just want to talk."

We picked up my things from the office and went out to the parking lot. When we got into the car, Karen reached over and squeezed my hand. "You've done good here. Cleaned up a big mess, and saved her career."

"She still has a tough road in front of her. She's basically on her own with two kids." I made a face and shook my head. "That ass-hole of a husband."

Karen leaned over and kissed me. "You can't fix everything. Anyway, I think she'll be all right now."

50

We drove home almost without talking, lost in our thoughts. We'd turned off of Route 1 onto Drakes Island Road before Karen broke the silence.

"I'm surprised that Claire Houghton didn't ask you to stay on as director. I'd have thought she would have wanted to keep you here until the new permanent director showed up. That's still several months away, right?"

"Actually she did ask, but I told her I needed to think about it. The candidate she had lined up as the new director backed out after hearing about all the crap that's gone on, so who knows how long it'll take for Claire to find someone permanent? At least six months to a year, and I don't think we want to be here that long. I'd really like to get back to my own lab, and I suspect shuttling back and forth between Boston and Maine would get pretty old for both of us."

Karen gave me a skeptical glance. "But can you really turn it down at this point? It feels like you'd be abandoning both Claire and MTRI."

"I know. And yes, I do feel guilty about that. Especially about deserting Carolyn and some of the other faculty members that I like."

"Couldn't you continue running your lab while you were director? You'd be able to spend more time in Boston, now that MTRI is out of crisis mode. Plus, you have Janet Klein there to help as your senior research associate."

I sighed. Karen was making it harder for me to decline. "Yes, I suppose I could keep things going. Janet's a big help, and people in the lab have gotten used to meeting with me by Zoom. But how do you feel about it? Are you up to traveling back and forth for another year?"

Karen shrugged. "I can handle whatever we need to do. It seems like it's important for you to hang in here. Besides, we've never really had the chance to enjoy Maine."

I laughed. "Maine hasn't offered us much in the way of enjoyment. It may be nice up here, but our visits have been pretty damn traumatic. Dealing with that monster Walter Monroe last year, and now a professional Russian hitman."

"Let's think about it for a bit. Are you in a hurry to give Claire an answer?"

I pulled the car up and parked in front of the Drakes Island house. "Not really. I'll just send Claire my report on Carolyn's tenure case with a note saying that I'll get back to her on the job in a week or so."

Karen smiled. "Sounds good. Any reason we can't take some time to ourselves while you're contemplating the directorship?"

"No, I suppose not. Why? What are you thinking?"

"Just that we haven't given Maine a fair chance. As you said, our visits here haven't been exactly fun. But now it's summer, nobody's trying to kill us, and we have a house on the beach. You know what they call Maine, don't you?"

I was starting to get her drift. But I said, "Murderland?"

She laughed and slapped me on the shoulder. "No, silly. Vacationland. And I think we should spend the week checking that out before we make a decision."

"Just hanging out on the beach enjoying ourselves? Sounds decadent."

"Yep. Rosie will love it. And we can take her for some nice walks, too. They have a one-mile trail that's open for dogs in the Rachel Carson National Wildlife Refuge and several short trails around the summit of Mount Agamenticus. The view from there is supposed to be spectacular. Plus, I've always wanted to see puffins, and there are tours that go out from Boothbay Harbor, just a couple of hours up the coast from here."

I laughed. "You sound like a tour guide. When'd you figure all this out?"

"I had to do something while I was waiting in your office during your faculty meeting. So, what do you say?"

I reached over and kissed her. "To a week of just playing around with you and Rosie? And seeing puffins? I'm all in."

Acknowledgments

I'm once again grateful to Alexandra Adams for her enormous help in critically reading and commenting on the manuscript. It's also a pleasure to thank Shrabastee Chakraborty for her careful reading and thoughtful suggestions. Their very kind and generous contributions made *Bad Medicine* a better book.

I'm also pleased to thank Kevin Poirier for introducing me to the ins and outs of Sanford, and Ulla Hansen for sharing her knowledge of sandpipers, puffins, and some of the financial aspects of contracts between pharmaceutical companies and academic institutions.

And, as always, my thanks to Audrey, Beau, and Patti.

About the Author

Geoffrey M. Cooper is a retired cancer researcher and academic administrator, having held positions at Harvard Medical School and Boston University as professor, department chair, and associate dean. He is the author of several scientific texts and is now using his experience in academic medicine as background for writing medical thrillers. He lives in Ogunquit, Maine.

Website: geofcooper.com

Reviews from readers are greatly appreciated. If you enjoyed *Bad Medicine*, please let other readers know by leaving your comments on Amazon or Goodreads.